False Cargo

SELECTED FICTION WORKS BY
L. RON HUBBARD

FANTASY
The Case of the Friendly Corpse

Death's Deputy

Fear

The Ghoul

The Indigestible Triton

Slaves of Sleep & The Masters of Sleep

Typewriter in the Sky

The Ultimate Adventure

SCIENCE FICTION
Battlefield Earth

The Conquest of Space

The End Is Not Yet

Final Blackout

The Kilkenny Cats

The Kingslayer

The Mission Earth Dekalogy*

Ole Doc Methuselah

To the Stars

ADVENTURE
The Hell Job series

WESTERN
Buckskin Brigades

Empty Saddles

Guns of Mark Jardine

Hot Lead Payoff

A full list of L. Ron Hubbard's
novellas and short stories is provided at the back.

*Dekalogy—a group of ten volumes

L. RON HUBBARD

False Cargo

GALAXY
PRESS

Published by
Galaxy Press, LLC
7051 Hollywood Boulevard, Suite 200
Hollywood, CA 90028

Printed in the United States of America.

ISBN-10 1-59212-267-1
ISBN-13 978-1-59212-267-7

Library of Congress Control Number: 2007903538

Contents

Stories from Pulp Fiction's Golden Age

A ND it *was* a golden age.

The 1930s and 1940s were a vibrant, seminal time for a gigantic audience of eager readers, probably the largest per capita audience of readers in American history. The magazine racks were chock-full of publications with ragged trims, garish cover art, cheap brown pulp paper, low cover prices—and the most excitement you could hold in your hands.

"Pulp" magazines, named for their rough-cut, pulpwood paper, were a vehicle for more amazing tales than Scheherazade could have told in a million and one nights. Set apart from higher-class "slick" magazines, printed on fancy glossy paper with quality artwork and superior production values, the pulps were for the "rest of us," adventure story after adventure story for people who liked to *read*. Pulp fiction authors were no-holds-barred entertainers—real storytellers. They were more interested in a thrilling plot twist, a horrific villain or a white-knuckle adventure than they were in lavish prose or convoluted metaphors.

The sheer volume of tales released during this wondrous golden age remains unmatched in any other period of literary history—hundreds of thousands of published stories in over nine hundred different magazines. Some titles lasted only an issue or two; many magazines succumbed to paper shortages during World War II, while others endured for decades yet. Pulp fiction remains as a treasure trove of stories you can read, stories you can love, stories you can remember. The stories were driven by plot and character, with grand heroes, terrible villains, beautiful damsels (often in distress), diabolical plots, amazing places, breathless romances. The readers wanted to be taken beyond the mundane, to live adventures far removed from their ordinary lives—and the pulps rarely failed to deliver.

In that regard, pulp fiction stands in the tradition of all memorable literature. For as history has shown, good stories are much more than fancy prose. William Shakespeare, Charles Dickens, Jules Verne, Alexandre Dumas—many of the greatest literary figures wrote their fiction for the readers, not simply literary colleagues and academic admirers. And writers for pulp magazines were no exception. These publications reached an audience that dwarfed the circulations of today's short story magazines. Issues of the pulps were scooped up and read by over thirty million avid readers each month.

Because pulp fiction writers were often paid no more than a cent a word, they had to become prolific or starve. They also had to write aggressively. As Richard Kyle, publisher and editor of *Argosy,* the first and most long-lived of the pulps, so pointedly explained: "The pulp magazine writers, the best of them, worked for markets that did not write for critics or attempt to satisfy timid advertisers. Not having to answer to anyone other than their readers, they wrote about human beings on the edges of the unknown, in those new lands the future would explore. They wrote for what we would become, not for what we had already been."

Some of the more lasting names that graced the pulps include H. P. Lovecraft, Edgar Rice Burroughs, Robert E. Howard, Max Brand, Louis L'Amour, Elmore Leonard, Dashiell Hammett, Raymond Chandler, Erle Stanley Gardner, John D. MacDonald, Ray Bradbury, Isaac Asimov, Robert Heinlein—and, of course, L. Ron Hubbard.

In a word, he was among the most prolific and popular writers of the era. He was also the most enduring—hence this series—and certainly among the most legendary. It all began only months after he first tried his hand at fiction, with L. Ron Hubbard tales appearing in *Thrilling Adventures, Argosy, Five-Novels Monthly, Detective Fiction Weekly, Top-Notch, Texas Ranger, War Birds, Western Stories,* even *Romantic Range.* He could write on any subject, in any genre, from jungle explorers to deep-sea divers, from G-men and gangsters, cowboys and flying aces to mountain climbers, hard-boiled detectives and spies. But he really began to shine when he turned his talent to science fiction and fantasy of which he authored nearly fifty novels or novelettes to forever change the shape of those genres.

Following in the tradition of such famed authors as Herman Melville, Mark Twain, Jack London and Ernest Hemingway, Ron Hubbard actually lived adventures that his own characters would have admired—as an ethnologist among primitive tribes, as prospector and engineer in hostile climes, as a captain of vessels on four oceans. He even wrote a series of articles for *Argosy,* called "Hell Job," in which he lived and told of the most dangerous professions a man could put his hand to.

Finally, and just for good measure, he was also an accomplished photographer, artist, filmmaker, musician and educator. But he was first and foremost a *writer,* and that's the L. Ron Hubbard we come to know through the pages of this volume.

This library of Stories from the Golden Age presents the best of L. Ron Hubbard's fiction from the heyday of storytelling, the Golden Age of the pulp magazines. In these eighty volumes, readers are treated to a full banquet of 153 stories, a kaleidoscope of tales representing every imaginable genre: science fiction, fantasy, western, mystery, thriller, horror, even romance—action of all kinds and in all places.

Because the pulps themselves were printed on such inexpensive paper with high acid content, issues were not meant to endure. As the years go by, the original issues of every pulp from *Argosy* through *Zeppelin Stories* continue crumbling into brittle, brown dust. This library preserves the L. Ron Hubbard tales from that era, presented with a distinctive look that brings back the nostalgic flavor of those times.

L. Ron Hubbard's Stories from the Golden Age has something for every taste, every reader. These tales will return you to a time when fiction was good clean entertainment and the most fun a kid could have on a rainy afternoon or the best thing an adult could enjoy after a long day at work.

Pick up a volume, and remember what reading is supposed to be all about. Remember curling up with a *great story.*

—Kevin J. Anderson

KEVIN J. ANDERSON *is the author of more than ninety critically acclaimed works of speculative fiction, including The Saga of Seven Suns, the continuation of the Dune Chronicles with Brian Herbert, and his* New York Times *bestselling novelization of L. Ron Hubbard's* Ai! Pedrito!

False Cargo

CHAPTER ONE

The Toughest Man Alive

SPIKE O'BRIEN'S bull bellow was deceptively hearty, gratingly cheerful. With one foot planted on the brass rail before the Honolulu bar, with a slopping glass of liquor tottering before his gross face, he roared, "Come on up here, every one of you sons! You're goin' to drink to the toughest man that ever sailed the Pacific. Snap into it, me buckos!"

A Kanaka-Chinese breed moved cautiously away, his black eyes bright with fear of the swaying bulk beside him. Spike O'Brien caught the movement out of the corner of his bloodshot eye. With a jerk of his thick wrist he sent both glass and liquor hurtling into the half-caste's face.

With a scream, the small yellow man clawed at his eyes and stumbled away. Blood was running down into his mouth from a cut jaw.

O'Brien laughed. The sound shattered even the noisy turmoil of the Honolulu dive. Men stopped and stared.

"Come up here, every one of you!" snarled O'Brien with a leer. "Come up here and drink to the toughest man on the Pacific. Spike O'Brien. S-P-I-K-E, Spike. O-B-R-I-E-N, O'Brien. The man who killed Shen Su. The guy who whipped the governor of Borneo. I'll take on any two of you—any three of you. I'll fight the whole damned bunch of you with both hands tied. Come on up here and *drink*!"

The fat barkeep stopped dispensing coolyhow and swabbed his greasy forehead. His eyes were pleading with someone, anyone, to do something about this. Men were stumbling up the steps that led to the dock street, deserting the place, trading its external and internal warmth for Honolulu's wet fog.

O'Brien turned around and swept his apparently drink-glazed eyes across the room and its remaining occupants. He was a tremendous bulk of a man, clad in black pea jacket, white-topped cap. His coat swung open and light fell on the brass buckle against his waist.

O'Brien's eyes rested on the far side of the room, went away and came back again. His mouth twitched with annoyance.

A white man sat there, quietly spinning a small glass between thumb and index finger. His hands were narrow and tapering as are those of an artist. His face was the face of a saint. His shoulders were of awesome dimensions, even though he was noticeably slender. O'Brien's annoyed glance rested on the quiet face, seeing only the fine features of a gentleman, completely missing the small light which danced far back in the metallic gray eyes. The face might be that of a saint, but the eyes did not match.

O'Brien did not like either face or fingers. He had ordered all up to the bar for a drink and this man had not answered the call.

"Hey, you!" barked O'Brien. "Come up here, unnerstand? You're going to have a drink with me whether *you* like it or not, see?"

The face showed very little interest. The small sparkling glass went round and round between the slim fingers.

O'Brien lurched away from the bar. The lurch was exaggerated. It took more than a dozen drinks to make Spike O'Brien that drunk. His eyes were suddenly cold, shining with an animal intelligence.

"You'll come up to this bar or I'll drag you up!" promised O'Brien, jolting against the table, spilling the other's glass.

"You annoy me, Mr. O'Brien. And I don't like your face. Get out of here before I change my mind about dirtying my hands on you." In spite of the import of the words, the quiet face did not change or show the slightest interest or emotion. The small lights in the eyes were flaring up steadily.

"You . . . you talk that way to Spike O'Brien?" O'Brien was plainly dumbfounded, aghast. He slapped his hairy hands down on the scarred top of the table and thrust his jaw close to the other's face. "Maybe—" said O'Brien, "maybe you don't know who I am."

"Probably not."

"Well, I'm Spike O'Brien, that's who I am. I'm the man Ring and Talbot brought all the way from China to do a job for 'em. I'm tough, get me? I'd just as soon *kill* you as look at you."

"Please take your face away," said the other mildly. "Your breath is bad. Haven't you any friends to tell you?"

O'Brien rocked back on his heels. His red-rimmed eyes focused on the other's face. His coarse lips moved soundlessly for a moment and then words exploded from them.

"Say, I know you . . . you're Brent Calloway!" he yowled.

The other nodded. "Yes . . . Brent Calloway. What were you saying a moment ago about being the toughest man on the China Coast? That scar on your jaw looks familiar, O'Brien."

The scarred jaw was jutting. O'Brien rocked on his heels, though he was plainly cold sober. He studied the other's position. A man sitting down makes a good target—he cannot dodge.

O'Brien's hand snapped to his belt. A short Derringer, smaller than the palm of his hand, capable of throwing two .45 slugs in less than two seconds, gleamed an instant under the hanging lantern.

Brent Calloway's fist disappeared under the lapel of his jacket. Flame blasted out from the table's edge. A second ribbon of sparks leaped up to scorch O'Brien's face.

The Derringer dropped with a clatter. A widening stare of surprise spread across O'Brien's coarse, flat features. His hands groped for the table edge. Abruptly he dropped, as though something had cut the string that held him up. The stubby fingers closed twice, and then O'Brien lay still.

Brent Calloway shoved the automatic back into his shoulder holster and glanced up at the entrance. Police might arrive any moment. All men had vanished from the basement dive.

Calloway stood for a moment staring down at the loosely sprawled form. A grimace of distaste passed across his face. Bending over, he thrust a hand into O'Brien's shirt and brought forth a packet of papers wrapped in a strip of oilcloth. Pocketing these, he walked steadily to the door and mounted the steps.

The fog closed in behind him.

O'Brien twisted about with a pain-racked grunt, finding just enough energy to shake his fist at the door and mutter, "This time you won't get away with it—not this time, Brent Calloway!"

CHAPTER TWO

Calloway's Masquerade

THE downtown section of Honolulu dripped in the dampness. The square white buildings were so many pale shadows behind the street lights. Streetcar rails were two small rivers running away through the mist.

Brent Calloway stepped into the protection of a doorway, glancing behind him. He struck a match to a pipe, and in the flare his lean, controlled face seemed longer. His tapering fingers sent the dead match spinning to the gutter.

Holding the pipe clenched between white teeth, Brent reached into his pocket and brought forth the packet he had taken from Spike O'Brien. Carefully noting that it contained a master mariner's ticket and letters addressed to O'Brien from Ring and Talbot, shipowners, he replaced the sheaf and reached into another pocket.

Bringing forth two sheets of paper, he opened one, slanting it out toward the street light. It was written on Lloyd's Underwriters' stationery and was addressed to himself at Shanghai. It read:

CALLOWAY:

Of course you can have a few months' sabbatical or whatever. But we would rather you made this affair company business. After all, as long as we are unable to put our fingers on Ring and Talbot, we stand to lose respect in the Pacific, to say nothing of hundreds of thousands in hull and cargo insurance. This underhanded business of scuppering ships for their insurance must stop.

But you realize, we are certain, the danger to which you expose yourself. We need not tell you that you are bitterly hated in Hawaii, that half a hundred men would enjoy shooting you down. It is therefore rather incomprehensible that you thrust yourself into this without apparent reason. But we have known you long enough to come to respect the Yankee logic behind your activities, even though we cannot quite understand at times.

Let us remind you, Calloway, that should you fail to get the *Barclay* intact to San Diego, your shrift will be short. That crowd would hardly hesitate to kill you. And we do not believe that you can possibly get that ship to San Diego.

You stated, further, that you also intend to locate the recently scuppered *Bolivia*. We remind you that the task of piloting the *Barclay* safely across the sea is enough for one try.

CHEERIO,
Ltd.

Calloway dragged at the pipe and refolded the letter, opening the second slip. This was a cablegram, also addressed to him at Shanghai. It was signed Dorothy Shannon. It said:

The *Barclay* will follow *Bolivia* at the hands of Mike Shannon's murderers. Please come.

Very carefully, Brent tore the two papers into small bits and went to the gutter.

The fragments fell, to be immediately swallowed up in the grate.

The building across the street bore the legend of Ring and Talbot, Shipowners. Brent entered, clattered up the rickety steps and thrust open the entrance of the outer office.

Inside the door was a railing of dark wood. Close against this was a rickety desk on which sat a dust-clogged typewriter. Papers were speared on rusty spindles. A picture of a schooner graced the dun-colored wall beside a metal filing case from which a handle was missing.

Brent took all this in at a swift glance and then looked at the girl behind the typewriter.

Her face was a study in ivory and teakwood, exquisitely carved. Her eyes were large and deep and black. Her dark hair caught and held the shimmering streams of light from above.

Brent said nothing. His gaze was level, a little surprised. The girl looked at him and crept back a little in her chair.

"Your . . . your business?" she faltered.

Brent came to himself with a jerk. "I beg your pardon. I didn't mean to stare. Are Ring and Talbot in?"

"Yes . . . yes . . . both of them." She rose and hurried to the inner door. "Who shall I say is calling?"

Brent's eyes were still on her face. "Spike O'Brien." He spat the words as though they were distasteful. His eyes were tense. But no sign of doubt came across the girl's face. Instead, her black eyes widened. She swallowed hard and thrust back the door.

In a moment she returned and nodded to Brent. He walked forward, and as he passed her she pressed herself as close to the railing as possible, as though afraid he might touch her.

For some unaccountable reason, Brent Calloway felt as though he had struck her.

In a welter of papers, charts, lading bills and cigar smoke, Ring and Talbot were waiting for him. Henry Ring was big and gaunt, with a yellow complexion, sunken eyes, and a vulturelike nose. George Talbot was in direct contrast to his partner. Talbot wore no coat, and his blue-striped shirt was almost black with dirt, surmounted by a celluloid collar over which hung the folds of his face. He needed a shave, and the gray bristles glittered in the light. His hair was almost gone, but those strands which were left stood in disorderly array above the narrow forehead.

Talbot, leaning back in his swivel chair and snapping a pair of once-white suspenders, spat out his cigar stump and said, "So you got here, huh?"

Ring stood up and gave Brent a limp hand to shake. The skin felt scaly.

"We've been waiting for four hours," said Ring in a creaking voice. "Waiting while you were out getting drunk."

Brent's watchful eyes studied them. His impassive, saintlike face did not change expression. "Can't a man get drunk if he wants to? If you don't like it, you know what you can do."

Talbot thumped both feet on the floor and leaned forward, jowls shaking. "Remember who you're talking to!" he commanded.

Brent reached inside his coat and brought forth a packet

wrapped in oilcloth. Looking inside, he selected a letter and threw it on the desk before Talbot.

"There's my identification," he said.

"Spike O'Brien," Talbot read. "Yes, that's all right." He peered back at Brent, raising his eyes and lowering his head. "I didn't think you'd look like you do, O'Brien."

"Are you saying anything about my looks?" demanded Brent.

"No, no!" hastily. "I thought from what we heard of you that you were a bigger man. I mean thicker and heavier. I'm telling you right now, O'Brien, that we ain't going to have anything to do with weaklings in our company."

"What's that?" snapped Brent.

Ring laid a hasty hand on Brent's shoulder. "He doesn't mean anything, Mr. O'Brien—nothing at all. It's just his way. Isn't it, George?"

"Humph!" George grunted.

"And now," said Ring, "won't you sit down, Mr. O'Brien, so that we can fully understand each other?"

Brent took a chair and sat on the edge of it, with his back away from the door.

Ring cried, "Miss Shannon!"

The outer door opened and the girl stepped nervously into the room. She stared at Brent, her white hands restless.

Ring's voice was peevish. "Look alive—don't stand there like a ninny!"

"What do you want?" said Miss Shannon bleakly.

"Humph!" said Talbot. "Tell her what we want, Ring. And make it plain, so she'll understand." Talbot chuckled.

Ring's creaking voice had an edge. "Get me the files on

13

the *Barclay* cargo. And I want the bills of lading, all of them, and the clearance papers we got this afternoon. Hurry!"

Miss Shannon closed the door softly behind her. A file case creaked in the outer room and presently she was back with her arms full of papers, which she deposited on Ring's desk. With another glance at Brent she went on out.

"Wonder she didn't bring in the telephone directory," Talbot grunted. "That girl's no good. Fire her as soon as I can get us another."

Brent, making his voice as casual as possible, said, "Where did you get her?"

"Her?" snapped Ring. "Get your mind off women, O'Brien. We've waited four hours to give you this, and I'm not going to wait any longer."

Talbot, with a glance at his partner, turned to Brent. "Don't pay any attention to him; he's nervous, O'Brien. About that girl, she's running around with Carter. We don't have any of that in these offices."

"But where did she come from?" said Brent.

"As if that made any difference!" said Ring.

Talbot shrugged. "Her brother was captain of the *Bolivia*, and after the *Bolivia* went down, his sister was left on the beach. Ring got softhearted and gave her a job."

"I didn't!" creaked Ring.

"You did!" Talbot snapped. "Gave her a job at ten dollars a week, and she's not worth fifty cents. Ring hired her, but I'm going to do the firing the next time she pulls something. If we fired her, we'd have to give her two weeks' pay."

Brent nodded. "The *Bolivia*—that's the cargo ship which went down off Mexico, isn't it? Lost with all hands. Only left some wreckage floating on the water. I didn't know it was your boat."

"Almost bankrupted us," whined Ring. "He didn't know it was our boat! But come on, come on, let's get at these papers!"

"Wait," said Talbot. "I hear Carter coming."

Ring muttered under his breath. Talbot went toward the door.

The footsteps had stopped outside and the low sound of voices filtered through the gaping cracks in the entrance. Talbot jerked the door open. Carter jumped back from the railing and glared first at Miss Shannon, then at Talbot. Carter's left cheek was fiery red. Miss Shannon stood back, staring at the floor, holding her right hand as though it stung.

Carter recovered his poise in a moment and entered the inner sanctum.

"Huh!" he said heavily, looking at Brent. "So this is the great Spike O'Brien! Hell, he doesn't look like he's so hot!"

Brent stood up and flexed his right hand. His eyes were fastened on Carter's left cheek. Carter laughed. Brent's right shot out and Carter slammed back against Ring's desk.

Brent resumed his chair and watched Carter gather himself up from the floor.

"Sorry, Talbot. I didn't know your friend hurt so easy."

Carter limited his attack to a ferocious glare. He was perhaps six feet two, and his raven-black hair straggled out from under the edges of a uniform cap. He was clothed in

15

muddy whites which were a crumpled mass of wrinkles. His mouth was a gash across his face.

Ring was pawing hastily through the papers. "Here, O'Brien. Here are the clearance papers for the *Barclay*. See, they're all in order. You can sail at dawn."

Brent took them and stuffed them into his pocket without a glance.

Ring went on. "And here are your manifests." He smiled, and the tightening of skin made his face a death's head. "Your cargo will be composed of sisal, for the most part. Hemp fiber, you see. For rope and—"

"Sure," said Brent. "I know what sisal is. I'm not interested in what I'm carrying."

"That's the right ticket," beamed Talbot, snapping his dirty suspenders. "You're not interested."

Ring nodded, gloating. "All right. Now, the first thing in the morning we will issue a statement to the papers saying that we have offered you a bonus of a thousand dollars for the safe passage to San Diego." He stopped long enough to beam again. "And here, in this manifest, you will find a typewritten sheet in a sealed envelope. These are your orders. You will open them at sea, and at sea only."

"And you're to go aboard immediately," said Talbot. "No drunken brawls tonight. We can't risk anything like that. No, indeed."

Brent's lean face was a little tense. His tapering fingers fastened themselves over the manifest and rolled it up. Far back in his chilly eyes, small fires flickered.

Turning to go, he looked again at Carter. "Beefsteak will fix your eye up, mister. Good night, gentlemen."

"A pleasant voyage," creaked Ring to the closing door.

In the outer office, Miss Shannon looked up and followed Brent to the entrance with her eyes. He stopped for a moment and looked back at her, then he was gone. A shudder passed over Miss Shannon's small back.

In the street below, Brent hailed a passing touring car which served as a cab. Climbing in, he studied the face of the half-caste driver.

"Park a few feet away from this entrance," Brent ordered. "And wait. There's an extra five in it for you."

The slant-eyed half-caste nodded and scratched his palm, sitting back to wait, little caring about the intentions of the man behind him.

A clock down on the docks struck eight times, mellow sounds which helped dispel the gloom. Brent sat far back, out of sight from the sidewalk. At length he heard the short stroke that signified that it was eight-thirty.

Rapid footsteps were coming down the stairs from the second floor. Small, clicking steps, half afraid. A shadow appeared in the doorway. Miss Shannon studied the street before her, her dark eyes restless. Certain, then, that nothing lurked in the darkness, she stepped out upon the glistening pavement and passed close to the touring car.

From the rear of the machine a hand shot out and clutched at her shoulder. The girl started to scream, but a second hand closed immediately over her mouth and crushed out the sound.

She was dragged forcefully into the interior of the car. Brent held her back against the cushions. Her defiant eyes burned into him.

"Drive!" barked Brent at the half-caste.

The machine moved away down the line of the docks. The street before the office building was quiet, deserted, quite as if nothing had happened. . . .

CHAPTER THREE

As the *Barclay* Plows East

SEA leagues had fled behind them, waves ranged the *Barclay* on either side, as though trying to match the steamer's speed. Far to the west a dark cloud was coming out of the night—a dark cloud filled with rain and wind.

Brent Calloway leaned against the bridge rail, staring moodily ahead. Beside him Chief Officer Monahan hunched a thick face into a dirty jacket collar, keeping a pair of washed-out eyes on Calloway's profile.

"That girl," ventured Monahan hesitantly, "is goin' to cause plenty of trouble, O'Brien. I never did like skirts on a ship, and now that Carter has the idea she's his particular dame, it—"

"I wouldn't worry myself if I were you," breathed Calloway with a quiet threat.

Hastily, "Oh, I didn't mean anything, O'Brien. I was just telling you where to watch out. As long as the frail keeps to the cabin it's all right, but you let this scurvy half-caste crew spot her much and it'll be just too bad. I know these guys, O'Brien."

"I'm sure you do," replied Calloway.

An occasional plume of dark spray lifted over the bows, spattering the anchor chains, to wash them bright. Down in the well deck, Carter paused on his way aft to look up and give the bridge an antagonistic smile. Calloway stared back, looking through Carter as though Carter was not there.

Monahan went on. "This old crock's not what we thought she was, O'Brien. She's got a bad engine. The boiler tubes are so damned rusty you could put your finger through 'em. I guess it doesn't matter, though."

"Why not?"

"Hell, O'Brien! You're not fooling anybody by keeping up that attitude. We know what we're here for. That is, all of us except that kid third mate and maybe the second engineer."

"So you don't believe," said Brent slowly, "that I'm taking us in to San Diego?"

Monahan snorted. "You ain't got a worry in the world, O'Brien—not one. I'm keeping up my mate's log to the hour. And it'll clear you. To hell with reports and clearance papers and what have you! They never worried me. The only reason I didn't get this job this time was because they took my ticket away from me six months ago. Been on the beach ever since."

"You'd better keep your log," said Brent in a tone which held a hint of threat.

"Don't get hot! We all know you're a plaster saint. There's them that would believe it, too, looking at your mug. Listen, here's what I want to know. When do I get rid of the third mate? Dayton."

"Who said you were supposed to get rid of him?" Brent still stared ahead, into the frowning blackness. He spoke in a monotone.

"Carter said so. But I thought I'd better talk to you. Who's in charge around here, anyway?"

"Don't ask that twice," said Brent.

"Okay—don't be so damned touchy! We're all in this together. Another thing. I'd like to know why the dame came along. She's not going to do anybody any good. She's a hothead, that one. Because of her brother, I guess."

"What about her brother?"

Monahan shot a quick glance at Brent. "Don't you know?"

"No."

"Guess these things don't get out to the China Coast. Young Shannon was the captain of the *Bolivia*. Didn't you hear," Monahan paused to laugh, "how the *Bolivia* went down with all hands?"

"Whereabouts did this happen?"

"Somewhere off Lower California. Big reports about it. Shannon was the captain of that ship. Worst day's work Ring and Talbot ever did when they hired him. He was chuck-full of Tradition and Duty and the Call of the Sea. Young squirt with big ideas. Bet they had a hell of a time with him. He looked like a fighter. And he didn't give up in a minute. Guess they had to kill him."

"Hard luck."

Monahan snatched at the wrong meaning. "Yeah. You don't want anything like that cropping out. This job is tough enough without it. Makes a man nervous. Often wondered how Carter ever managed to get back."

"So Carter was aboard the *Bolivia*, eh?" Brent sounded a little bored.

"Sure he was. General handyman for the R. and T. Don't anything slip up while Carter's around. No, sir. He's a man

21

that'd go through with anything. I'd hate to meet up with him in a dark passageway."

"Sure. Fine man. Fine man."

"But R. and T. thought they needed you for this job. Guess you weren't slow about taking it, either."

"Why so?"

"Aw, don't be like that, O'Brien! Relax! You're among pals—we're all in the same stew. I guess you think I don't know about the Yanks getting you for gunrunning a couple of months back. News has a way of getting around. And don't tell me you weren't plenty glad to be able to give them the slip, either. And how about that killing in Chefoo last spring? Those three British officers you knocked off. Stuff like that gets around."

"I guess it does," said Brent.

"And it cost plenty to buy your way out, didn't it? Only one man you never could buy."

"Who was that?"

Monahan grinned evilly at Brent's profile. "A friend of mine."

"Didn't know you had any friends, Monahan."

"Yeah? Well, there's one guy that's nobody's friend, too. At least nobody in this racket."

"Who's that?"

"Brent Calloway."

Brent started violently and whirled on his chief officer. Brent's hand was already creeping up to his shoulder holster. His eyes were shot with a deadly flame. Monahan jumped back, cringing.

22

"Wait! Wait!" begged Monahan. "Don't shoot!"

"So you know Brent Calloway! Know him well?"

"No, no, no! Honest-to-God, I don't, O'Brien! Honest-to-God, I never even laid eyes on him! I was just joking, that's all. Can't a guy joke a little bit? Listen, O'Brien, listen. I—my God, don't shoot!"

"Tell me all about what you know of Brent Calloway," said Brent in a hard, monotonous voice.

Monahan, finding himself trapped in a wing of the bridge, straightened a little, his shoe-button eyes wild with fear. He saw that the helmsman had not noticed.

"I'll talk," he said. "I'll talk. What do you want?"

"You heard me the first time. What do you and the rest of this outfit know about Brent Calloway?"

Monahan held hard to a stanchion. "Only this, O'Brien. He almost got you once. Shot at you, they say. I was just having a little fun with you."

"Start at the beginning."

"How . . . how . . . why . . . ? Brent Calloway is a—"

"Go on."

"Hell, you know all that!"

"Go on!"

Monahan wilted. "I don't blame you for hating him, O'Brien. They said that he was right in Honolulu when we sailed. Said that he was going to try to get you. He hates our kind. He came in from the China Coast on the *President Monroe* two days before you came third on the *Empress*. A buddy of mine recognized him as he came down the gangway. I'm just as anxious as you are to see him bumped off. I was just kidding when I said he was a friend of mine. I was just being sarcastic.

"This Carter wants to get hold of Calloway. He says he's got reasons of his own. But there don't seem to be many who know his face. There's some more of us that would like to get him, too. He wouldn't last very long if he was on this boat. You're among friends, O'Brien. There's not one of us that wouldn't like to see Calloway dead. The crew is saying something about him. They're afraid that he'll pop up and scupper this deal and throw us all in the brig. We know what he did to Shanghai Trans-Oceanic when they went bad. Most of 'em are dead.

"The gang's afraid because this pal of mine spilled it that young Shannon once worked with Calloway. They were mates together on the *Hong Sing*. And they're afraid that this Calloway'll pop up like a bad penny and scuttle the lot of us. One feller said today that he wouldn't be surprised if Calloway had tried to get aboard this hooker. We looked all around at the crew, but we couldn't see anybody. If he is aboard, O'Brien, you can depend on us. We'll kill him before he can squirm. We'll look after you all right. And I'll guarantee that I'll be the first to shoot."

"Why didn't you bring this talk to me sooner?" demanded Brent.

"Because we know all about you, that's why. We're afraid you'd start shooting before we could explain that we meant right. I know how a feller can get in your ratlines that way. When I heard I lost my job because Calloway had uncovered some evidence after the wreck, I said right then and there that I'd shoot him on sight. And there are others in this hooker that'll be just as glad. They were with me, some of them."

Brent took his hand away from his left side and turned back to watch the plumes of spray and the lowering sky.

"So you'd shoot him on sight," he murmured.

"Sure," said Monahan, suddenly hearty. "And you can go right on saying that about landing us in San Diego. We know what the score is, O'Brien. You're not laying yourself wide open by talking out loud, but if you want to be mysterious about it, go ahead."

Monahan started to go away. He frowned and came back, putting his face close to Brent's. "But I wouldn't talk too loud, O'Brien. Some of the boys might take you serious and knife you some dark night."

"Some of the boys?"

"Most any of them. And another tip, O'Brien. Watch this man Carter. He's going to try to murder you and do the job himself. Jealous. And he wants that bonus. Ten thousand dollars is big pay just for killing a man, O'Brien."

"And if Carter killed me," said Brent with an acid smile, "you could assume command and kill Carter. Then who would get the ten thousand?"

Monahan, seeing that Brent's fingers were far away from his left side, nodded with a knowing air, edging away. "I'll let you figure that out, O'Brien. I'll just let you figure that out!"

Monahan was lost in the shadows of the boat deck. A wave shattered itself against the *Barclay*'s bow, burying machinery, tarps and hatch in a greenish white smother of froth. Wind whined plaintively in the sparse rigging—not unlike the scream of a banshee sensing death. . . .

CHAPTER FOUR

Eight Bells—and Trouble

A T eight bells on the third night out, Jimmy Dayton, third mate of the *Barclay,* clattered up the bridge ladder and strode across the deck toward Brent, who stood at the rail watching the restless black sea.

Dayton saluted smartly. He was about twenty-five, lanky, full of the sureness of his breed. "My trick, sir."

Brent nodded. "Right. Watch yourself, Dayton. There's more than a blow brewing."

"What do you mean, sir?"

"Pass it up. If anything happens, I'll be either in my cabin or at the radio shack. Where is Miss Shannon?"

"She's in the new cabin you assigned her, sir. Next to yours."

Brent moved away. "Right. Don't let anything happen."

He went aft along the boat deck toward the radio shack. The rain marched along before him, polishing the sooty deck.

The Portuguese-Japanese-Kanaka was leaning over his key, his teeth and nails glistening. His black beady eyes were intent upon the blank bulkhead before him. The earphones were crackling.

"What's up?" Brent demanded.

The operator was startled. He wheeled in his chair and shot his fingers to the switchboard beside him.

"Stop!" said Brent. "If you're that anxious to keep something in the dark, I'd better find out about it."

27

But the operator had already thrown the switch. The generators died down, their sound immediately replaced by the whine of wind through the rigging.

"Get up off that chair!" ordered Brent.

The third-caste operator's nostrils flared angrily. Whipping off the earphones, he jumped to his feet. "Not so fast, O'Brien! You may be master of this ship, but you're in here now. This is my place!" He stabbed tense fingers toward his hip pocket. A gun appeared as though conjured out of thin air.

Brent snatched at the wrist. The operator winced and cried out sharply. Writhing, striving to free his gun hand, he aimed a kick at Brent's shins.

Brent's left hand gripped at the gun muzzle. With a side twist, he secured the weapon and in the same motion hurled the operator backward. He got up, sullen, his eyes burning.

Holding the gun loosely, Brent studied the breed's face. "Now just *what* was the idea of that?"

"You can't pull anything like that on me, O'Brien! I'll have Carter down on you!"

"I'm scared to death. Get out on deck and look at the weather. I'm going to play with your toys for a little while."

Sullenly, the operator retreated. Brent slammed the door, battened it, and closed the port with its steel plate. He turned to the set. The operator had not had time to change the wave setting. It was only necessary to connect the receiver.

Sitting down, Brent laid his cap aside and pulled on the headphones. A rattle and crack of static greeted him. His expert fingers sharpened the dial setting.

With a side twist, he secured the weapon and in the
same motion hurled the operator backward.

The static blurred out, to be immediately replaced by a QST. Brent threw in the generator switch and turned to the key. He noticed that the broadcaster was not set on its prescribed band.

"Okay," rattled Brent. "Go on."

The headphones took up the staccato chain of dots and dashes.

"Okay. Repeat. Crew getting sullen under long wait. Anxious to know when you'll be back. The B is low on provisions and liquor. Can you pick up something for us? Please give us your position."

Brent's pale gray eyes grew hard. Throwing the switch, he tapped, "Position not available. We'll have plenty for you, don't worry. What is your position?"

He listened for a full minute for the answer, but the air was empty of all save static. Finally he took off the phones and replaced his cap.

"They're wise," he told himself. "And B would mean *Bolivia*. And the *Bolivia* is supposed to be under the waves this long time."

A heavy fist was pounding on the door. Brent threw off the catch.

Carter was there, his flat, ugly face dripping with rainwater, his gash mouth drawn back to display his teeth.

"What the hell's the idea, O'Brien? You go messing around like that much more and you'll wake up and find yourself dead. I won't stand for anything like that, get me?"

"I get you—I more than get you." Brent looked past Carter

at the operator. "And if I had any sense I'd throw both of you into the drink. Only Davy Jones would have to have a strong stomach to stand you." He brushed past them and strode back to the bridge.

Carter sputtered, almost too mad to swear. He caught the operator by the collar and thrust him to the key. "You half-wit! You left this thing tuned in, and he's wise!"

"I can't help it," whined the third-caste. "If you think—"

"Shut up and take a message." Carter slammed the door and crouched over the operator's head like a line squall. "To Ring and Talbot, Honolulu, TH. Have reason to believe—"

"Not so fast!" whined the operator, his pencil flying.

"Have reason to believe something wrong about captain. Check everything. Contact police and steamship companies. Waiting for immediate reply. Carter." He scowled at the closed door. "And if you're not O'Brien—" He patted the gun butt which protruded from his pocket.

The operator nodded grimly and rubbed his twisted wrist. "O'Brien never would have had the brains," he muttered. "He sends like a regular. I told you, Carter—"

"Shut up, and get that off!"

Brent entered his cabin and threw his cap on the bed, deep in thought. His eye caught a movement beside his desk and he whirled about. Then he relaxed and smiled.

"Good evening, Miss Shannon. Like it better up here with the gentlemen?"

"Well enough, Captain O'Brien." Dorothy Shannon stood

up, holding to the edge of the desk. Dressed as she was in a dark blue serge sport suit, she seemed unusually pale. Her dark eyes—a throwback to those far days when the shattered Spanish Armada had been cast up on the Irish coast—were a little scornful.

"I think," she continued, "that the time has come to speak of many things."

"Shoes and ships?" asked Brent, stuffing and lighting his pipe.

"No—of rats and ships. I want to know what you intend to do with me."

"Well, now that you speak of it, I don't think I've given it a thought. Haven't things been decent enough for you?"

"Oh, they've been decent enough. What with Carter cat-footing about trying to catch me alone, and you staring at me for minutes at a time, and with the crew saying all sorts of things about why I'm here—what I want to know is this. Why *am* I here?"

"Oh, I wouldn't be able to say right off the bat. The *Barclay* didn't look so good, and I thought maybe a beautiful lady would improve the appearance of the decks." He took a long drag at the pipe and then shifted it into the corner of his mouth. His lean face was almost expressionless, but his eyes were humorous.

"You have placed me in an embarrassing position, Captain O'Brien. I cannot be certain that you will land me in San Diego. I don't know what you intend to do with either the ship or myself. Your orders were to sink this boat in mid-ocean."

"And the *Barclay* still bobs like a cork, eh? To tell the truth, Miss Shannon, I'm rather uncertain about your ultimate fate."

Her hand whitened as she gripped the desk. "Perhaps it would be better if you made up your mind. I have a friend, a very powerful friend."

"And who might that be?"

"A man by the name of Brent Calloway. If anything should happen to me, he would seek you out to the ends of the earth and destroy you."

Brent Calloway smiled. "Interesting. How long have you known this Calloway fellow?"

"He was my brother's best friend. And now that Mike Shannon is dead, I know that Brent Calloway will track down and discover his murderer. And should anything happen to me, that will only be one more reason for Brent Calloway to take the trail."

"Have you ever seen this fellow?"

"No, but I have heard about him through my brother. And I know that he has heard about me."

"Then if he's never met you, why do you think he would take any interest at all in your case?"

"Perhaps I believe in such a thing as chivalry, Captain O'Brien, a quality which must be quite foreign to your nature."

"And this Calloway seems to be chivalrous, that it? Now I happen to know that this fellow killed a good many of the men of Shanghai Trans-Oceanic when it went bad. That makes him a killer. And I know that he interferes with lawful enterprise. That makes him a thief. Thief and murderer,

Miss Shannon. And you think he'd cross an ocean to rescue a beautiful lady!"

"He has done it before," she contested, her face flushed with anger. "The things he has done had to be done. They meant either his life or another's. You cannot blame a man for self-preservation. I cabled him a month and a half ago. I told him that the *Barclay* was about to be scuppered as the *Bolivia* was. He'll search you out, O'Brien, and if you harm me, it will only be another reason for him to kill you. But perhaps if you treat me well, give me safe conduct, then I may be able to intercede for you with him."

"Will you intercede for Carter?"

"You're laughing at me!" She flung back the door and stepped defiantly into the passageway.

When the door slammed, Brent knocked out the bowl of his pipe and grinned. "So Brent Calloway will get me if I don't watch out!" He seated himself on his bunk and refilled the pipe. "Crazy," he murmured to himself. "Going stark crazy. In another minute I'd have gone gunning for Brent Calloway myself. In fact, maybe I ought to."

Leaning over on his side, he began to pull off his sea boots. With one halfway removed, he grinned and leaned back. "If I play O'Brien much longer, I'll be O'Brien. As my old dad said, there's such a thing as being too thorough."

Removing the boot and dropping it to the deck, he paused again. "Hell, maybe I *am* O'Brien!"

The gold watch on his wrist sparkled in the light. Grinning, he took it off and turned it over.

On the underside, letters had been engraved, almost too fine to be read.

The inscription said, *Brent Calloway, for valorous service in our behalf. Lloyd's Underwriters.*

"No," sighed Brent. "Unless I stole this thing from Calloway, I'm still Calloway."

Someone was pounding on his door and he hastily replaced the only identification he ever carried. . . .

CHAPTER FIVE

Brent Meets the Showdown

FIVE days out from Honolulu the blow was still strong. The sea had faded from a bright bottle green to a somber gray. Waves raced alongside the *Barclay,* matching the height of the rail—white-capped waves battered by the howling wind.

The *Barclay* stood it well enough, but the men suffered. The crew was sullen, independent, obeying commands only after minutes of bullying. They obeyed then only because they could see Brent on the bridge. They thought too much of Spike O'Brien's reputation to press matters far. They had not even taken him a sample of their food—a time-honored feeler, used by sailors to test the metal of their master.

Quartered on the bridge, Dorothy Shannon was growing easier as to her ultimate fate. She had seen nothing untoward in O'Brien's attitude. In fact, she thought she had detected some slight sympathy.

Hands thrust into the pockets of her bright slicker, Dorothy Shannon went forward to the wheel. Jimmy Dayton and Brent were talking together in the shelter of the chart room. Their backs were toward her and they did not know that she could hear them.

Brent was bending over a chart, juggling a compass in his slim fingers. "We're right here, Dayton. And we're supposed

37

to be over *here* according to the owners." He marked another spot further to the south.

Dayton shook his head. "I don't see anything wrong with that, sir. We're on the course all right."

Brent smiled at his third mate. "Forget it. Did you make that cargo inspection for me?"

"Yes, sir. I've been at it all morning."

"What did you uncover?"

"Why, sisal, of course. It's all in order, according to the manifest. Just bales and bales of sisal, still in good condition."

"Sisal? That doesn't seem right. You're certain that you looked at the underside bales as well as the top?"

"Dead certain, sir. I know sisal."

"But damn it!" said Brent. "That doesn't check!"

"What do you mean, sir?"

"Forget it. Better go out and see if that half-wit helmsman still has us on the course."

Dayton stepped out and almost collided with Dorothy Shannon. His cheeks colored, and he hurriedly touched his fingers to his cap, immediately stepping away as though on very important business.

Brent saw Dorothy at the same time. "Come in out of the wet."

She entered and perched herself on the table edge. "I heard what you said. I'm sorry that I eavesdropped, but—"

"That's all right. I'm glad you did. I wanted to see you about it."

"Why me?"

"Because you're the little lady that's supposed to know all about these things. At least you told me that you did. Now please tell me why this ship is loaded with real, number one sisal instead of rocks or maybe a couple barge-loads of plain mud."

"I didn't know it really had sisal in the hold."

"Don't try to sidetrack me. If you know the answer, speak up. If you don't, I'll tell Brent Calloway on you."

She shifted uneasily at mention of the name and quickly returned to the subject. "I . . . I thought you knew all about this business."

"I haven't even opened those sealed orders." Brent tapped his jacket pocket. "Are you sure you don't know anything about all this?"

"Well, I know—or *think* I know—what's been happening."

"In as few syllables as possible, tell me."

She studied his face, a little puzzled. "All right. Ring and Talbot are making a practice of buying up ships which are about ready for their annual insurance inspection. It would cost too much to repair the hulls and engines, so they get them cheap. And they don't want to repair the hulls and engines themselves, so they load up with a cargo or two and send it around just to make it appear that they're on the level.

"But on the third trip, perhaps the fourth, the ship gets into a bad blow. It's lost at sea. And Ring and Talbot collect the cargo and hull insurance without any objection whatever. And that's what is supposed to happen with this boat."

"Then why would the hold be filled with real sisal?"

Dorothy shook her head. "I'm sure I don't know."

"This sinking ships for their insurance is the oldest racket in the world. I guess maybe the Phoenicians tried it. You're sure now that this is the case?"

"Certain. That's how . . . how Mike Shannon was killed."

Brent frowned. "I suppose, then, that the insurance people didn't like to let her go without a thorough inspection. And Ring and Talbot, after the *Bolivia* disaster, were forced to load a real cargo this time."

"Why are you so interested in the reasons behind the case?"

"Oh—I like to know what I'm doing. A man only gets hung once, you know."

"You mean hanged."

Brent smiled. "No, Miss Shannon. I'm afraid that hanging is too good for Spike O'Brien." He stepped to the bridge where Dayton was watching both helm and the seas ahead.

"I haven't seen Mister Monahan around for quite a while, sir," said Dayton. "He's supposed to take some watches, isn't he?"

"Yes, he's supposed to," Brent agreed. Taking his pipe out of his slicker, he crammed it with rough-cut tobacco and lit up. The blue cloud was immediately dispersed by the wind. Only a sailor can light a pipe in a high breeze.

"And I haven't seen Carter since he went back to the radio shack some time ago." Dayton did not seem worried. He wanted to talk more than anything else.

A premonition surged through Brent, but he pulled three times on the pipe before he replied. "So he's in the radio shack! I wonder what news the air might be bringing in."

40

Dayton glanced over Brent's shoulder. "There's Carter, now."

Brent turned slowly. Carter, Monahan and the radio operator were entering the bridge from the well deck. They had the appearance of pallbearers—or perhaps executioners. Something in the way they walked suggested the manner of the Inquisition priests marching to the stake and the victim in the auto-da-fé.

Carter's gashlike mouth was spread in a sardonic, humorless smile. He stopped, and Monahan and the operator swung into line beside him.

"Get off this bridge," said Carter.

Brent looked the three of them over, taking a full minute for the scrutiny. "Perhaps you had better follow your own order," he said.

"Don't act tough, me bucko," growled Carter. "We're smart all of a sudden. You're pretty good—pretty damned good—to keep us guessing for five days. But that's all over. You didn't fool *me*."

"A fool is hard to fool," Brent remarked. "How does all this come up?"

"We radioed Ring and Talbot. We radioed them to find out if you were on the up and up. After we sailed, a guy named O'Brien looked Ring and Talbot up, but they didn't believe this guy until we radioed. You're all up, all washed up, Brent Calloway. And we're your personal executioners."

Dorothy Shannon's white face appeared in the charting room door. The quietness of the proceedings only heightened the ice-cold quality of her danger. When Carter said

"Brent Calloway," Dorothy Shannon's eyes widened with sudden understanding.

Brent pulled on the pipe. "And so you think you're good enough to get me, that right?"

Monahan laughed and looked down at his fingers, which he clenched viciously.

"Good enough," said Carter. "Plenty good enough. We're wise to the works now, and there's only one thing to do—kill you and throw your carcass to the sharks. But before that happens, I want to tell you that I certainly appreciate your bringing this Shannon dame aboard. It'll relieve the monotony. Thanks, Calloway."

The operator's bulging teeth glistened. "I've sent an SOS. We're sinking, see? And what would be better than to put your corpse in a lifeboat and set it adrift with a lot more wreckage? That ought to look convincing."

Monahan spat on the deck. "Hell, why talk? Let's give it to him!"

Carter reached into his waistband and jerked at the butt of a .45. The operator backed away toward the rail, tugging at his own weapon. Monahan laughed and started to reach down.

Brent took a drag at the pipe. Simultaneously, his right hand lashed up to his left breast. The crash of the shot was dull in the gale. Blue powder smoke and blue tobacco smoke clashed.

The operator went rigid. The gun he held tried to stay level. Monahan fired. A gash appeared in the paint behind Brent's back.

Brent sent a carefully aimed slug at Monahan's chest. Carter

42

plunged for the companionway, aware that he was alone even before Monahan was dead.

The operator still teetered, held up by a stanchion alone. The man's gun was steadying, his eyes narrow with painful concentration. Brent fired at the bulging teeth.

The radioman was hammered back. The gun flew straight up. Like melting snow, he sagged over the far edge of the bridge.

A curling wave closed over the body.

Monahan was coughing and twisting on the red-spotted planks. The *Barclay* rolled steeply and Monahan slid suddenly down to the scuppers. He lay very still.

Brent put away the gun and turned around, pipe still sputtering between his teeth.

"Get on the wheel," was his quiet order to Dayton.

CHAPTER SIX

Disaster Strikes
the *Barclay*

A few sea miles were all that remained between the *Barclay* and San Diego. But the miles were storm-harried and overcast with inky darkness. The sharp stinging flurries of rain made vision difficult. It was almost impossible to see the bow from the bridge—and no lookout was in the bow.

Brent's hands were tight upon the wheel, Brent's eyes stung with unwavering watchfulness. Dorothy Shannon was beside him, watching the bridge ladders, listening for the sounds of a possible attack. In command of the bridge alone, Brent knew that the engine room was still under his orders. Not because the engineers were loyal, but because dead engines in this squall would mean nautical suicide. Without the storm he would have been helpless.

Something dark and round soared up a companionway and thudded against the planking. Brent dodged. Dayton scrambled out of the chart room and scooped the object into his sea-hardened fist.

"Uh!" grunted Dayton. "It's a note tied to a belaying pin."

Brent handed the wheel to the mate and unfolded the paper. The water-smudged pencil marks were difficult to decipher, but the signature was clearly Carter's.

"The crew thinks we ought to give you a chance," said the

note. "If you'll turn over the bridge, we'll put you in an open boat. Otherwise, we'll blow you apart as soon as we reach our destination. And I get the Shannon dame, no matter what you do. Think it over."

Brent pocketed the note.

"What is it?" demanded Dorothy.

"A lot of damn foolishness," Brent said. "Watch those ladders."

She nodded and Dayton relinquished the helm. The *Barclay* plowed on toward San Diego, through the converging shipping lanes, buffeted by mountains of black.

Brent knew what Carter could do, but he did not think Carter would try it. If Carter did . . .

"What did the operator mean about an SOS?" demanded Dorothy Shannon.

"According to that, we're reported sunk. They'll find some wreckage on the water the way they did with the *Bolivia*. And if I fail to get this ship into San Diego, the crew will be officially dead."

"Then what about the *Bolivia*?"

"She's still afloat—somewhere. I don't know what this is all about. We have a real cargo when we should have a few hundred tons of rock. We're ordered to scupper a ship, which is scuppered on the records only. Someone in this deal is getting the double cross."

"The triple cross," said Dorothy. She stared up at his face, his lean, hard, reposeful face. Her mind was not on Brent's remark. She was thinking that Mike Shannon had been right in everything he had said about Brent Calloway. She was thinking that Mike Shannon would like to be here tonight, instead of . . .

Brent was speaking again. "No radio. Nothing to bring help if anything goes wrong. Well, maybe we'll make it—and maybe not. I hope so. Say, Miss—Dorothy. Did the inspectors check the *Bolivia*'s cargo?"

"Why, yes, they did. And they checked this one, too. Ring said that somebody had tipped them off. I don't know why that would be. Nobody wanted to have to carry a real cargo. It was that much money lost in the scuttling. Can't we radio, Brent?"

"No. They cut off the juice on us."

"Then that's out. They've cut our speed down, Mr. Calloway. Will we be in tomorrow morning?"

"I guess so. If we're not, we'll be in a pretty bad way."

"Well, suppose we run into another ship or pile up on the beach?"

"Then I'm afraid that Carter and his crowd would have us between the thumb and forefinger."

"But we have command of the boats that remain."

Brent shook his head. "If anything happened, I suppose I'd be enough of a fool to let them have the boats rather than let them drown. Here. Take this wheel a moment. I'm going to check our course and take a look aft."

Dorothy Shannon laid her hands on the spokes. For an instant her fingers lay against Brent's wrist. Then he was gone.

She saw him lean over the rail and stare aft. Evidently everything was all right, because he went immediately into the chart room and bent thoughtfully over the charting table.

"Take this wheel a moment.
I'm going to check our course and take a look aft."

Something was happening to the spokes under Dorothy's hands. The ship lunged giddily into a trough and rolled out, shaking water like a dog. The second pitch carried the *Barclay* broadside to the seas. She heeled over at a forty-five-degree angle. Waves smashed over the bridge. The ship's lee rail was all the way under.

Dorothy Shannon cried out, throwing her slight weight against the helm. The lee rail stayed under. It was fifty to one that the top-heavy, carelessly loaded tramp would work her way further down. In another instant the vessel would capsize.

Brent came struggling up the deck, holding to a line. He was shouting, but the words were lost in the thunder of water. Brent reached the binnacle and clung to it. Cargo was shifting all through the ship. Unbattened chairs were roaring across the cabins, smashing themselves against the bulkheads. A cargo boom swung loose and threshed out like a wielded club, finally thrusting its tackle into the waves.

Brent snatched at the spokes and tried to pull up on them. For a moment nothing happened. All life seemed to hang suspended at forty-five degrees.

It was as though the wheel had snapped. The lower edge whipped the water.

Brent shouted into the tumult, "She's gone! The cables have gone!"

Dayton struggled toward them, mouth tight. He did not look back at the waiting sea.

Dorothy gripped a stanchion—seemingly the only solid thing in an awry world. A pair of binoculars shook themselves loose from a peg in the windward wing and flashed toward her. Missing her by inches, the field glasses slashed into the water and disappeared.

A degree at a time the ship began to right herself, shuddering, bouncing, yawing, like a wind-buffeted gull. It was as though the *Barclay* had pulled her lee rail out of mud. Abruptly the port side swooped toward the dark sky. The reaction sent the windward rail down, but not under. Back to the leeward again.

In a few seconds, the ship was heading diagonally across the crests, picking up knots with each passing minute.

Gingerly, Brent felt of the wheel. It swung to and fro at the slightest touch. And yet the compass was holding to a new number and holding it well.

It took Brent some minutes to understand what had taken place. He walked restlessly along the rail, staring down at the water as though it would tell him the underlying reason.

Brent's face was altogether too calm when he came back to Dorothy Shannon and Dayton by the wheel.

"They've got control," said Brent dully. "They must have disconnected the chain tackle from these cables to the rudder posts aft. They're steering by the big three-man helm back on the fantail."

"Then we've lost control of the ship!" cried Dorothy.

"We've lost control," Brent replied. He glanced into the compass and made a rapid calculation. "We're heading south-southeast, down the coast of Lower California."

"But why?" demanded Dayton.

"I was a fool," Brent said. "I thought I knew what the

game was all about, but I guess I've played my cards wrong somehow. Officially, we're all dead. The ship is dead. Lloyd's will have to pay up for loss of both hull and cargo.

"Meantime, we're heading for the most desolate section of the North American coast—Lower California, Mexico. God knows where! And when they get us where they want to go, it won't be hard to starve us into surrender. They know who I am. They'll want me for reasons of their own. You, Dayton, sided with me. That accounts for you."

Dorothy Shannon looked back at the compass, her dark eyes wide and anxious. "And then Carter . . ."

Brent, with a surge of anger, remembered how she had had to slap Carter that day in the office.

Through night as black as ebony, through waves that made a toy of the *Barclay,* they plunged onward into the south. Brent watched the compass disc.

It gave him an eerie feeling, that disc, staying in one place as it did. It was unnatural to be on the bridge of a ship without being in command. Of course, Carter was steering from the poop deck—steering with the big auxiliary wheel which is on every ship. But that was a blind spot. Carter was trusting to compass alone. No lookout forward, no thought to possible stranding.

And Carter had more faith in his own navigation than a scanty training would warrant. Blissfully unaware of the major dangers that might lie ahead when they entered the Santa Rosita Islands, Carter deviated not an inch from his set course.

Occasionally Brent touched Dorothy Shannon's arm, as though to make certain that she was still there. Something in the touch sent a small vibration up to his mind. It was like sipping a strong liquor. Evidently she sensed his concern for her, for her face was turned up to him whenever he was near.

Dayton strained his eyes into the thick blankness that lay before them. Occasionally he muttered a seamanlike oath to himself, as though he could project his anger back to the poop deck.

Suddenly Dayton gripped the railing with both hands, his face rigidly held by something he had seen.

"My God!" he cried. "There's a light! A light dead ahead!" Whirling, and cupping his hands, he bellowed, "Port your helm! Light dead ahead!"

But the words were drowned in the smothering, howling wind. Brent clamped tight teeth on his pipe stem, staring into the opaque spray and night. The light came again, more plainly. It was gone in a space of seconds.

"It's not a buoy or a lighthouse," muttered Brent. "It flares up."

Dayton started toward a ladder. "I'm going aft and—"

"You're not going anyplace," rapped Brent. "They'd kill you for your pains. Better stand here and take it."

"But that's land!" cried Dayton. "We're running straight at the beach at a fifteen-knot clip. It's a fire, I tell you!"

"What if it is? If they beach her, that's the end of my hopes of getting her into San Diego. Lloyd's will have to pay up, fraud or no fraud. There's nothing wrong with the insurance."

STORIES from the GOLDEN AGE

☐ Yes, I would like to receive my **FREE CATALOG** featuring all 80 volumes of the *Stories from the Golden Age Collection* and more!

Name

Shipping Address

City   State   ZIP

Telephone   E-mail

Check other genres you are interested in: ☐ SciFi/Fantasy   ☐ Western   ☐ Action/Adventure

FREE SHIPPING!
NO PURCHASE REQUIRED

10 Books • 15 Stories
Illustrations • Glossaries

10 Audiobooks • 20 CDs
15 Stories • Full color 40-page booklet

Fold on line and tape

IF YOU ENJOYED READING THIS BOOK, GET THE MYSTERY COLLECTION AND SAVE 25%

BOOK SET	AUDIOBOOK SET
$99.50 **$75.00**	$129.50 **$97.00**
ISBN: 978-1-61986-093-3	ISBN: 978-1-61986-094-0

☐ Check here if shipping address is same as billing.

Name

Billing Address

City   State   ZIP

Telephone   E-mail

Credit/Debit Card #: _____

Card ID # (last 3 or 4 digits): _____

Exp Date: _____/_____ Date (month/day/year): _____/_____/_____

Order Total *(CA and FL residents add sales tax)*: _____

To order online, go to: **www.GoldenAgeStories.com** or call toll-free **1-877-8GALAXY** or 1-323-466-7815

www.GoldenAgeStories.com

To sign up online, go to:

1-877-8GALAXY or 1-323-466-7815

7051 Hollywood Blvd., Suite 200 • Hollywood, CA 90028

GALAXY PRESS

COLLECT THEM ALL!

STORIES from the GOLDEN AGE

by L. Ron Hubbard

Brent found nerve enough to smile. "I guess Brent Calloway will presently be out of a job."

The gold wristwatch ticked unheard into the roaring gale. *For valorous service . . .*

"They can't help but spot it," said Dorothy Shannon. "They can't! They must be blind!"

"They're steering from the poop deck," Brent reminded her. "And no lookouts forward. Let 'em pile her up. Let 'em smash her all to hell. I'm to the point where I'm about ready to enjoy one swell, splintering wreck. The harder it hits, the better I'll like it."

A little amazed, the girl stared up into his face. There was nothing wild in Brent's expression, nothing hysterical in the way his teeth clamped that dead pipe. Suddenly she found that she could understand his sentiment. Let them pile her up once and for all, and to hell with the whole sickening business!

The hands of the gold wristwatch were at two minutes past four. Presently they read three minutes, then four minutes. *For valorous service in our behalf.*

Dayton's mouth was tighter than a trap. Rage, more than fear, burned in his eyes. He had a seaman's hate for the wanton destruction of a ship. After all, a ship seemed a live, human thing. She carried cargoes and people to ports over the world. She was an indispensable connecting link. She was the key to glorious adventure and, again, the means of gaining the lowest strata of life. She was human. She was inhuman. But more than that, she had a personality which either drove you to exhaustion or lent wings to your feet.

And a ship was about to die.

Brent knocked the ashes out of his pipe bowl and reached for his pouch. "You'd better get some life preservers," he said. "You may have some swimming to do before long."

"What about you?" demanded Dorothy.

"I'd rather do my own drowning. Besides, the thing would cover up my holster."

The reddish light was steadily visible now. Occasionally Brent thought he could see the separate flames. Ominously, the waves had lessened, until they rode on an almost even keel.

A new sound was in the air. The thunder of a surf breaking before them. Soon the line of white would be visible, and immediately after that—

"Damn them!" muttered Dayton. "Damn them!" He said it in a dead monotone. "They ought to know!"

The line of white was visible through the rain. Surf dead ahead. Brent looked up and saw that the false dawn was at hand. The clouds were parting in the east, letting through thin rays of gray, yellow light. Mountains were faintly discernible—purple shadows not yet defined.

The keel hit with a shattering, grating snarl. The *Barclay* lunged over on her side and leaped back. The stern carried half around, geysering white spray. Torrential sheets of water poured over the fo'c's'le head and slashed, boiling and angry, against the bridge.

Brent was knocked sprawling against the rail. He was up instantly, pipe still gripped in set teeth. His hands were searching through the welter of foam.

"Dorothy! Dorothy!"

For an instant he thought that he had found her. But it was Dayton, struggling to his feet, swearing.

"Where's Dorothy!" Brent cried. "I had her arm, and then—" He saw the torn spot in the windbreak and jumped to it. Boiling sea was below.

Men were screaming through the ship. Steam hissed through the engine room fidley. The *Barclay* was beginning to settle, lifted by the outer reaches of the surf. The beach was more than a hundred yards away from them.

Dayton pulled at Brent's arm. "Come on, jump! She's liable to slip back!"

Spray-filled air gripped them. Brent felt himself going down, down, down. Was there never any end? He kicked, and beat the water with his hands. His lungs were hot coals in his chest.

CHAPTER SEVEN

Into Spike O'Brien's Hands

BRENT CALLOWAY stumbled up the beach, leaving long indentations in the white sand. Through the blackness behind him, cries blasted the night. Orders were immediately given and disputed. Shrill shrieks of fear were cut off short. Davits were creaking as the lifeboats from the topside were lowered, askew, into the foaming, ebon outer surf. The *Barclay*'s carcass made a gigantic shadow against the graying sky.

Brent searched through his pockets and found his soggy pipe. Clamping this firmly between his teeth, he turned his face toward the spot where he had seen the beacon sputter.

"Well," he told the surrounding darkness, "Ring and Talbot won. And I lost—perhaps more than I know."

A man was stumbling just ahead of him, swearing as he groped through the tumbles of rock. It was Dayton. When he saw Brent, Dayton swore in a louder, heartier voice and fell in behind.

The beacon was still flaring up, spreading a red glow through surrounding shrubbery and boulders.

"Ahoy!" came from dead ahead. "This way, me hearties!"

Brent stopped, removed the pipe, and replaced it in the corner of his mouth. He seemed a little shaken. In a moment he strode forward into the lighted area.

For a half-minute Brent regarded the lean, black-haired,

black-eyed man before him. The stare was returned. Dayton, knowing that something was up, stood back, waiting.

Brent went ahead, holding out his hand. The other took it very calmly, shook it and let it drop.

Brent's voice was noncommittal, almost flat. "Hello, Mike."

Mike Shannon grinned. "Hello, Brent."

Although they had not seen each other for years, although one had thought the other dead, although their youth had been shared cruising the China seas, they said nothing more than that.

Brent cleared his throat. "Your sister—Dorothy, you know. Your sister was aboard the *Barclay*."

Mike Shannon's bright eyes went dull. His grin faded as though it had been whipped away by a mighty hand. *"Was?"*

"Maybe . . . maybe she'll turn up, Mike. You never can tell. She could swim, couldn't she?"

"Yes." Mike looked back at the sea. "Maybe we hadn't better stand here by this fire. There's quite a lot of shooting going on. I got away from the *Bolivia*—she's anchored around the point in a harbor—but they aren't satisfied with marooning me. I've got too much on them. Mutiny, barratry, et cetera. Guess we'd—"

The whiplash crack of a revolver smote the blackness. A log jumped out of the fire, scattering sparks. A leaden slug whined like a plucked banjo string.

The three dived in behind a rock. Mike Shannon raised his black topknot over the edge. Another bullet snapped.

"I didn't want to see you go up on the beach, so I built the fire when I spotted your running lights," said Mike.

"Who's that doing the shooting?"

"I dunno, Brent. *Bolivia* bunch, I guess. They're all through these woods tonight. Spent the afternoon looking for me. It's gotten to be a sort of game."

"Then," said Brent, pulling on his cold pipe, "they'll have left some boats up on the beach near the *Barclay*."

"Heavily guarded," supplied Mike.

"What the hell?" shrugged Brent. "Let's go!"

They slipped into a ravine and worked down it, keeping low. Dayton, not able to feel the sudden change in Brent—a change occasioned by Mike's presence—followed the two, his mind far from comfortable. Dayton liked to fight things he could stand up to and swat. And his gun was down in the Pacific somewhere.

The edge of the beach came unexpectedly. Suddenly the *Barclay*'s riding lights appeared through the ink. Shadows were moving between land and sea—shadows along the beach.

Brent whispered in Mike's ear, "All we do is sprint up and bat the first one over the head. Then we take his gun and crack down on the rest. Then we get a boat, go out to the *Bolivia*, take it over, crack down on Carter and his crew, and sail the *Bolivia* to San Diego."

"That's all," said Mike.

Brent dug in his toes like a sprinter at the starting line. One shadow was bulkier than the rest, thicker. Brent eyed it uneasily. It might be—but it couldn't be! He'd have to find out.

"Ahoy!" roared Brent.

Mike gave vent to some wild Gaelic war cry. Dayton supplied the first of the Seven Great Sea Oaths and supplied it loudly.

Like an avalanche, they burst from the shrubbery and catapulted toward the water's edge.

Brent's shadow whirled. Light streaked along steel. Brent struck and felt his quarry go down. Mike entangled another boat guard. Dayton was on his third Great Sea Oath.

Sparks and bullets began to flame from the right. A fusillade of shots rapped from the left. Brent grabbed the bow of a cutter and leaped inside. Something human was before him. A rifle strap cracked as the weapon was swung down. Brent's left arm was numb. The rifle strap cracked twice and Brent staggered back, falling down into the edge of the surf.

Mike was bellowing. The rapid, sharp cracks of fists on flesh were heavy. Dayton was not swearing now.

A gigantic tower stood over Brent. Arms were encircling him in a mangling grip. His heels dragged as he was carried up the beach.

A flashlight came into play, casting a restless beam along the sand. First it picked up Dayton, lying in a loose heap at the edge of the trees. Then it caught the white, angry face of Mike Shannon as he struggled vainly in the confining hands of three seamen.

And last it rested on Brent's face. Brent sat up and fished through his jacket, pulling out the pipe and inserting it in his bleeding mouth.

"Well, me buckos," said Brent, almost cheerfully, "I suppose that that is that. What's next on this evening's broadcast?"

"You'll find out what's next!" promised an ugly, rumbling voice.

A sailor came up with a lantern and set it down. The

60

yellowish light shone upward into a heavily matted beard, into a pair of slitted eyes, against a brass buckle which was exposed by the open front of the pea jacket.

Brent grunted, "Hello, O'Brien."

"Oh, so you remember me, huh? So you remember Spike O'Brien! And don't forget, me bucko, that you've got to deal with the toughest hellion that ever sailed any one of the seven seas. You got to deal with me, Spike O'Brien!"

"Well, well and well!" said Brent. "How'd you get here? Swim?"

"Naw. You were so damned slow getting here, that I had plenty of time to grab a fast boat to Dago, grab me a fast car down here and then a speedboat out to this island. You're not half as smart as Spike O'Brien, Calloway."

O'Brien turned to the sailors. "Tie these guys up good, get me? Tie 'em up so it hurts and hurts plenty. Then you can throw 'em in the hold out on the *Bolivia*. We'll let the rats chew on them tonight. You seem to like rats, Mister Calloway."

Brent sighed and reset the pipe in his mouth. Mike Shannon's eyes were black, spinning with impotent rage. Dayton was moving, very feebly. As he tried to rise, O'Brien slammed a hard sea boot into his ribs and he lay back, lay very still.

O'Brien laughed and waded off through the sand in search of Carter.

CHAPTER EIGHT

Where Hell Begins

IT was dark and musty, wet and odorous in the hold of the *Bolivia*. Sisal was stacked about in mammoth piles. At least the fiber was soft to lie upon, even though it made a fiendishly cutting set of handcuffs and leg irons.

Twelve hours in one position was tedious and numbing. After the first hour, Brent had had no other sensation than the tingle of blood-robbed limbs.

Thumps had come from the steel-plated decks above them, punctuated by the screaming whine of cables through rusty blocks and the hammering, hissing protest of a donkey engine.

Mike Shannon's voice was weak from lack of water, and pain. "They're loading something, Brent."

"Wouldn't kid me, would you? That's the sisal from the *Barclay*. I'm suddenly in the know about all this."

"What about it?"

"They were ordered to scuttle both your ship and mine, but they didn't follow their orders."

"They tried hard enough with the *Barclay*."

Brent grunted. "That was just punk seamanship, lad. They had a use for the *Barclay*. Carter was with you on the *Bolivia*, wasn't he?"

"Sure," said Mike, giving the word an Irish twist.

"All right. Carter came back to Honolulu in time to be in on the *Barclay* deal. He must have had some correspondence with O'Brien on the matter, because O'Brien knew right where to find the *Bolivia*.

"Mike, they intended to leave enough wreckage floating to make matters convincing. Then they intended to bring both ships down here out of sight. After that, they're going to peddle all this sisal into Mexico. Mexico has sisal, too, you know. And they have a use for the boats."

"But," said Mike, "how did the R. and T. let real sisal get on these boats?"

"Carter tipped the inspector off and then tipped off Ring and Talbot. That way he was certain to have a cargo he could sell. Now, then. They take these boats—or rather this boat—over to the mainland, bribe the spiggoties to register them. Then they reinsure, take the ships out and get the *dinero* all over again. They cut Ring and Talbot out of the second deal.

"This isn't barratry, it's double barratry. And the false cargo is the sisal, instead of sticks and stones."

"Shut up," said Mike. "Somebody is coming."

Dayton unexpectedly spoke up. "Yeah. O'Brien—"

"If," murmured Mike, "we could only find out what happened to Dorothy!"

Spike O'Brien's elephantine steps and bull bellow put a stop to any further thought or speech. "All right, me buckos, come on up and get yourself some air!" His gross, putty-plastered face bore a mirthless grin. "Did you have a pleasant night?"

Sailors swarmed down the steep ladder and fastened hard

hands on the three, bearing them upward as though they were so many sacks of coal.

Brent was slammed sharply down on the deck and a sailor knelt with a clasp knife and severed the bonds which held his wrists. Brent gave his wrists a tranquil study and then began the work of rubbing the circulation back into them. That done, he fumbled in his blue jacket for his pipe, found it, stuffed it with rough-cut and looked up at O'Brien.

"Got a match?" said Brent.

O'Brien glared. His great sea boot shot upward, struck the pipe bowl, and sent both pipe and tobacco scattering across the dirty planks. That done, O'Brien seemed to be in a much better humor.

"Now," he rumbled, tramping restlessly back and forth, "I got to think how I'm going to put you guys out of the road."

Brent's eyes met Mike's. Dayton began to swear. O'Brien looked back at the cabins along the boat deck and scowled. Pulling a very black slice of cut plug from his pants, he gnawed a mighty segment and began the noisy work of reducing it to a soggy pulp.

"Now I'm thinking that you guys don't know about my having your dame up there," he said finally.

"You mean—" began Mike.

"Yeah, that's what I mean. We fished her out of the drink last night, and as soon as she spotted a cabin, she jumped in and locked the door. It was my cabin. If you can see that forward port there, you can see her face."

Brent's face jerked upward. There in the circle of glass

he could see something white. On closer study, he could recognize Dorothy.

"She won't come out, see? And she's got the fancy idea she can jump over the side when we ain't looking and get ashore. She thinks she can get away from Spike O'Brien. Do you get my idea, Carter?"

Carter was sitting on the hatch cover, his gash of a mouth wreathed into a twitching smile. "I get you, O'Brien."

"Naw, you don't! You're not smart enough to keep up with Spike O'Brien. You think she's yours, don't you, Carter? That's a laugh, me bucko—that's a great big laugh! That dame's mine. God knows how long we'll have to stay out here in this place!"

Brent looked at Mike and then up to the port.

O'Brien went on, pointing a dirty finger at Dayton. "Take that guy and pass a line under his arms, understand? Then shoot the line over the crosstree and belay it."

Two sailors leaped to do O'Brien's bidding. Dayton let them have a blue broadside and squirmed. They held him down and carried out the orders. In a moment, with three men pulling on the rope, they had lifted Dayton five feet in the air.

O'Brien swaggered up to the bridge ladder and stepped outside Dorothy Shannon's place of refuge. "Hey, you in there! See that guy dangling? Well, I'm going to hoist him up until he's fifty feet off the deck. Then I'm going to saw the rope in half. If you want to watch it, stay in there. If you don't, come out. But I'm going to repeat on all three, if you act funny!"

No sound came from within the cabin. Dayton's eyes

fastened on the boat deck each time he came around from a complete whirl. There was something gruesome about the way Dayton spun.

O'Brien tramped down the ladder and marched across the planks to the line fastened at the rail. Pointing to it, he said, "Haul away!"

The three sailors hauled, hand over hand. Dayton went upward, jerkily. The five feet became ten, the ten thirty, the thirty increased to fifty, and Dayton was almost touching the crosstrees. The hard deck was far beneath his swinging, spinning feet. He looked down at O'Brien and glared.

O'Brien grabbed a clasp knife out of a sailor's pocket and held the knife against the rope.

Looking up at the cabin, O'Brien roared, "I'll give you three to come out. After that I start cutting!"

He waited a moment and then roared, "One!" No motion of the cabin door. "Two," bellowed O'Brien. "*Threeee!*"

The razor-sharp clasp knife began to saw at the rope. Fifty feet overhead, Dayton's eyes were losing their glare. Dayton knew that he was already a dead man. But he did not beg for mercy. He knew that he was only a pawn to a larger scope of play.

One strand went, twisting as though in agony. A second began to part. Dayton was lowered a foot. He spun like a top.

The cabin door crashed back. Dorothy Shannon, attired in sailor pants and white shirt, gripped the bridge rail. "Stop!"

O'Brien turned around, grinning. He spat and cleared his throat. "Okay, sweetie. Come on down here if you ain't got the guts to stand it."

Reluctantly, her eyes fastened fearfully upon the swinging body high above them, Dorothy came down the ladder. Her great dark eyes were wide with fear.

O'Brien clamped his mammoth paw over her wrist and jerked her close to him. "Now, you're talking, see? You going to be good to me?"

Dazedly, staring up at his face with disbelief, trembling with both anger and fear, she shook her head in the negative.

O'Brien reached out with the clasp knife. The blade bit into the rope. There was a sharp crack. Dayton screamed.

Turning with agonizing slowness, falling with rocket speed, he came through the fifty feet of space. The scream ended as his body crunched into the deck.

A small trickle of blood ran from Dayton's crushed face.

Dorothy Shannon backed away, sobbing, groping for support.

"Now," said O'Brien, very businesslike. "We'll string up Mister Shannon and see to it that you give me your word."

"My God, no!" she wailed.

Mike Shannon's usually swarthy face was the color of wood ashes. His lips were tight together and his eyes were filled with white fires.

A sailor, looking at Dayton's quiet body, backed away, one foot at a time. He was less than a yard from Brent. And in that sailor's pocket were a clasp knife and a revolver.

Two men grabbed Mike's shoulders. Another line was passed under Mike's armpits. Another man heaved a belaying pin through the air and over the crosstree. O'Brien watched with a delighted grin.

*O'Brien clamped his mammoth paw over her wrist and
jerked her close to him. "Now, you're talking, see?
You going to be good to me?"*

• L. RON HUBBARD •

Dorothy Shannon's mouth was slightly open, as though she were suffocating.

Brent looked at O'Brien, and then at Carter. Neither was watching him. Experimentally, Brent hitched closer to the knife and the revolver.

They were passing the line to the rail, securing it. Three men laid hold eagerly and began to pull. Mike was jerked five feet off the deck.

Brent's face was very calm. His long, tapering fingers caressed the gun butt. He tightened his hold, pulled and rolled away.

The revolver barked. The rope which held Mike was neatly cut in two. At ten feet, Brent couldn't miss. Mike slumped to the planks.

Brent opened the knife and slashed the ropes which held his feet. Then, with an expert throw, he sent the knife quivering into the deck a foot from Mike's face. Mike's hand was about the hilt. The sharp blade was biting into Mike's bonds.

O'Brien roared and started to charge Brent. Then O'Brien saw the black tunnel, saw that it centered his thick chest. He stopped.

Brent felt in back of him and located his pipe, which he clamped between white teeth. "Now, if you gentlemen will please—"

A belaying pin soared out of nowhere and caught Brent on the jaw. Another brass pin struck him in the back. Mike Shannon was on his feet, swinging a block and tackle. A skull cracked and a man went down.

Brent dizzily tried to rise. He saw O'Brien rushing at him. Somehow he couldn't lift the gun. He saw the knife in O'Brien's hand.

A small foot came into play. O'Brien tripped and sprawled on his face. Dorothy Shannon snatched Brent's collar and towed him toward the fo'c's'le.

Wielding the lethal block and tackle, Mike fought a swift and complete rear-guard action.

The fo'c's'le door slammed behind them.

CHAPTER NINE

The Loser Pays

A bullet cracked through the panel, splintering it. Another slashed through the glass in the port, spreading out a fine spray of sharp slivers. Brent wiped away the blood from a small cut on his face. Dorothy Shannon hugged the far wall. Mike stepped to the door and glanced out through the gash.

"They're getting a boom to batter this down!" said Mike.

"Can't stay here," agreed Brent. "Pull up that hatch ring—and stay low." He tore up two beds before he found a revolver. With this in hand, he motioned Dorothy and Mike into the narrow, foul-smelling hatchway.

Three sailors arrived with the hastily dismantled boom. They crashed the end of it into the panel. The man in the lead dropped his end of the wood and whipped a knife from his belt. Brent dropped him. The sailor sprawled through the opening, still trying to wield the knife.

O'Brien's voice was loud above the increasing din. "In there after 'em. Get 'em out or I'll have your hides! I'll show 'em they can't get away with anything on this ship!"

Mike was motioning frantically from the steep ladder, only his head and hand visible. "What you waiting for?"

"A shot at O'Brien!" snapped Brent.

Overhead, footsteps were resounding. A hatch on the fo'c's'le head began to slide back. A man's face jutted through the opening, bearded, evilly intent. Brent sidestepped. A knife quivered in the deck where he had been an instant before. Brent fired hastily, still moving.

He leaped for the companionway and scrambled through, seeing Mike ahead of him. From the dark of the hold, Dorothy Shannon's voice was begging them to hurry.

They went on, rounding bales and tripping over boxes. Behind them the pack gave cry. Brent stopped as they neared the midship section and emptied his gun at the following shadows.

A great oval door was in front of them. Mike unfastened the heavy battening lugs and slipped through.

It was as though they had suddenly walked into hell. The fireroom, its heat built by that of the spinning sun overhead, was more than a hundred and thirty degrees. No wind was in the ventilators to act as a cooling measure. The boilers further aft were under pressure, furnishing steam for the winches which had been used to load the *Barclay*'s sisal.

From above them came the stamp of hurrying feet. Brent stared up at the fidley and saw running men. The maze of grates above their heads were protection against hastily fired guns, but the men were not stopping to shoot. They were too certain of their quarry.

From the after section, eager fists were beating open the engine room hatches. A medley of shouts came from the direction of the bow.

Mike looked hastily around him. "We're trapped!"

"And out of ammunition," added Brent.

A dozen men were swarming down the engine room ladders.

Brent reached up and took down a fire hose. Glancing at the boiler behind him, he saw a steam valve. In an instant he had coupled the hose to the valve.

Holding the brass nozzle, which he had wrapped with waste, Brent shouted, "Give her hell, Mike!"

Mike spun the wheel. The sizzling rush of steam—live steam, scalding hot—filled the boiler room. A gigantic geyser of withering mist sprayed upward, through the grates.

Men screamed and tried to draw back. But the steam could travel faster than men. They clutched at their throats, tried to cringe back, sought to escape the inevitable plunge through space.

Like shot gulls they plummeted down from the ladders.

The men who came from forward stopped and tried to retreat. But they, too, had not realized what scalding fluid can do. The full impact of the lashing stream struck them. They wilted to the scorching plates.

Through the gyrating white fog of heat, Brent swung around to the control station. Mike, understanding without being told, shoved Dorothy out of the way and opened the oil feeders into the fireboxes. The glutted flames roared under the onslaught of forced fuel.

Brent pulled the throttles, port and starboard engines. The *Bolivia* lurched, tugging at her anchor chains. The mighty links writhed under the lunging of the propellers. Loud cracks came from the forward deck.

Unable to get at his wheel in time, O'Brien had been forced

to slip his anchors to keep from going on the beach. The *Bolivia* wheeled under the stress of the starboard propeller. Steering cables screeched as the wheel was put hard over.

Brent reversed his throttles. Once more the *Bolivia* wheeled.

"Keep doing that!" Brent shouted at Mike. "I'm going up and get O'Brien!"

Brent leaped up the ladder three rungs at a time. He burst through the outer engine room door and raced for the bridge.

"Get him!" roared O'Brien from the bridge, and turned the wheel over to Carter.

Brent made the bridge ladder. Bullets rattled like hailstones on the steel before his face. He soared up the ladder and dashed into the wing.

O'Brien stood with sea boots planted wide apart, gun in hand. He fired point-blank at Brent's head—but Brent had already changed his position.

Brent angled for a direct shot. O'Brien fired a second time. A leaden hand twitched Brent's sleeve. Brent raised his revolver, slowly, calmly. O'Brien let out a startled bellow and whirled, running down toward the starboard ladder which led to the well deck.

Carter's hand was shadowed by his gun muzzle. The weapon flared, but Carter was too excited for the niceties of shooting. Brent did not so much as move. Knowing that he could take care of O'Brien in a moment, he centered his sights on Carter's shoulder and let drive. Carter slumped, trying to hold himself up by the wheel.

The *Bolivia* was headed out to sea. Brent yelled down the

engine room speaking tube, "Keep her on a straight course with those throttles." He did not wait for Mike's reply.

Possessing himself of Carter's gun, Brent clattered down the bridge ladder, down the companionway that led to the forward deck.

O'Brien was halfway across the deck. Not expecting Brent's rush, O'Brien shot too late. His gun went sailing out of his hand and into the sea, and Brent carried him back with a savage charge. Bawling with sudden fear, O'Brien made for the ratlines.

Brent could have shot him at that instant, but instead he threw down the guns and grabbed for the rope ladder that led up to the mast crosstrees.

O'Brien looked back and did not see the guns. With a sudden roar of understanding he stopped and tried to stamp on Brent's hands. Brent snatched at the ankle of a sea boot and jerked. O'Brien, shaking free, went up the ratlines like a great hairy baboon.

Two sailors came from the fo'c's'le. One raised his revolver, aiming for Brent's side. Squinting his weather-washed eye in heavy concentration, he pulled the trigger.

Brent sagged. For an instant he did not think he could hold to the ladder. The deck was already thirty feet below him. He gritted his teeth. Somehow the feel of the pipe stem helped. But the stress was too much for the hard rubber stem. It snapped and the bowl went spinning through space, to shatter itself on the planks.

The sailor started to fire a second time. But the report

did not come from the fo'c's'le. It came from the hatchway under the bridge. The sailor dropped, supported himself for a moment and then collapsed.

The spell of dizziness passed and Brent tried to go on up. O'Brien was now far above him and O'Brien's hands were busy with something—Brent could not quite see. The ratlines were swaying as though twisted about by a mighty wind.

And then Brent knew what was happening. O'Brien was unscrewing the lugs which held the ratlines to the crosstrees. And if those lugs were gone, the ladder would collapse and Brent would be catapulted to the deck.

Mike Shannon fired a hasty bullet at O'Brien from the hatchway, but the range was too long. Brent clutched the tarred cables. The wound in his side was numb, terrifyingly numb.

His blurring eyes caught sight of something shiny on his left wrist. A watch face. And below that face were the words *For valorous service in . . .*

Trying to breathe, trying to hold on, Brent made himself inch upward. One half of the ratlines sagged. Only one bolt remained.

The ticking of the watch was loud in his ears. *For valorous service . . .*

Brent made another crossbar. The watch threw back the sun's rays, shattering them in a glorious burst of gold.

For valorous service . . .

Another rung.

O'Brien's laugh was loud, strained. "You will try to buck me, huh? You'll try to buck *me*, Spike O'Brien, the toughest—"

Down on the deck, Dayton's untouched body was a small, pitiful huddle.

For valorous service . . .

Brent's side was beginning to hurt—as though he were being branded. Another rung. He could see the laces on O'Brien's German sea boots. He could see the blur that was O'Brien's body against the glaring sky.

The beach was sliding past them. The carcass of the *Barclay* bobbed and shifted in the surface as though nervous at the thought of being left alone and dead in this forgotten harbor. Something clicked in Brent's mind as he saw that. Somehow he found time to think that he might be able to float the *Barclay* on this high tide.

The creak of the bolt was loud in his ears. A fraction of an inch at a time, the ratlines were shifting downward, sagging.

O'Brien's voice was deafening. ". . . Spike O'Brien, the toughest man in the Pacific!"

Brent's white face was oddly smooth. It bore the look of wondering surprise rather than agony. His metallic gray eyes were narrow with concentration.

The ratlines sagged again. Brent reached out with his left hand and caught at the platform. O'Brien's sea boots came down on his fingers, hard.

Brent felt the ladder leave him. His legs were dangling over fifty feet of space. The deck below was somehow inviting. It looked soft and white from this dizzy height. He swung there like a pendulum.

O'Brien's sea boot landed a second time. Brent held on. His

right hand went out, fumbling. The stamp had set O'Brien slightly off balance, but it was enough. When Brent's fingers fastened on his ankle and pulled, O'Brien did not realize what was happening.

"So!" roared O'Brien. "You tangle with me, huh? You tangle with Spike O'Brien! You thought—"

O'Brien raised his foot for another crushing heel blow on Brent's left hand. Brent's fingers jerked a second time.

Caught off balance, O'Brien cried out, his bellow rolling across the ship. He clawed for a hold on the topmast, but his fingers, greasy and short, could find no purchase.

Space engulfed him. He turned over once, twice. The planking seemed to rise to meet him. His bellow was cut off. The sound of his striking body came back up to the crosstrees.

Someone below cried out.

Dayton's body moved slightly, influenced by the gentle roll of the *Bolivia*. But it was uncanny, as though Dayton had grimly nodded his approval.

Spike O'Brien's crushed hulk did not move. Not anymore, ever.

Brent awoke with a feeling of annoyance. Someone was pressing a glass to his lips, someone had a hand under his shoulders, raising him. His eyes flickered open and the annoyance vanished. Dorothy Shannon, with a certain air of ownership, was looking down at him.

The pleasant feeling her eyes gave him vanished in its turn. His side was a burning hell of pain. He sank back, very tired.

Almost an hour later, Brent was aware that Mike Shannon was there beside him. He found enough energy to say, "Everything . . . all right . . . Mike?"

"Sure it is, old-timer. Sure it is. You'll be surprised just how all right everything is."

"I know, but . . . I hated to . . . to lose the *Barclay*."

Mike grinned. "You didn't, Brent. Devil a bit of it, old boy. If you had strength to sit up, you'd be seeing the *Barclay* skimming along behind us as pretty as a gull."

Brent's eyes shot open. *"What?"*

"Sure. We floated her on a high tide. She's just as good as ever, Brent. Just as good as ever. Now you lay back and get some sleep. That wound isn't dangerous, and it'll get plenty of attention in San Diego. Just smashed some ribs, that's all."

"That's all," agreed Brent, trying to smile.

Dorothy Shannon was shoving her brother away. "Get out, Mike. He needs rest."

She took Brent's hand and seated herself on the edge of the bunk.

The wristwatch was almost hidden in bandages, but before he went to sleep, Brent saw the golden case. That and the shattered remnants of his pipe, lying in state on the top of a chest.

81

Grounded

Grounded

I had heard a great deal about the man, as all of us had there on the China Coast with little else to think of other than another's troubles and our own, but I was not prepared for the slim, handsome fellow who stepped through the night and fog from the customs jetty into the gig I had piloted from the HMS *Spitfire*. As it was a cold night, he had drawn his Navy cloak up around his throat to stave off the dampness of the Huangpu mist, and his correct bearing and manner of dress reminded me of a Nelson or a Frobisher, rather than the murderer and coward I had come to meet.

He stepped into the cockpit of the gig and, after a hesitant moment, extended his hand toward me.

"I am Lieutenant Hampden," he said, haltingly.

"Ensign Reynolds, sir. At your service." He seated himself on the low seat and I gave the cox'n his order. The engine began to sputter as the waves slapped at the exhaust and we moved away from the jetty.

As he made no further attempt at speech, I remarked, "I hope you will like the *Spitfire*, sir. The captain is ill at the moment, and I presume that you will have to take her upriver in the morning."

"I hope I will be able to like her, Ensign." He turned his head and gazed back across the river at the receding Bund.

I knew that this was his first trip to China, but he didn't seem to be looking at anything in particular. The lights of the Bund were dim and blurred with fog, but the noise of Shanghai came to us even over the spitting and gurgling of the exhaust behind us. A junk swerved by, a huge dark bulk of rotting wood. I could see her painted eye half-submerged from excess cargo. I started to point out the fact to the lieutenant, but noticing his preoccupied air, I held my peace.

The *Spitfire*, as tasty a little ship as ever graced the fleet of His Majesty the King, lay well up the river, and as the stream slipped past and we dodged in and out among countless steamers and men-o'-war, I fell to thinking on this strange new executive officer she had inherited. At the first glimpse of him, I had been forgetful of the thousands of wagging tongues which had told Shanghai of his disgrace, but now that I sat beside him and saw him in the uniform of the British Navy, I was loath to believe all those vicious tales I had heard. I suppose the uniform had a lot to do with it, for the love of service is bred deep in the sons of the academy.

I had heard of Lieutenant Hampden six months before at the start of my China cruise. The papers had been full of him and how he had won a famous racing cup for speed flying. He had been in the Royal Air Force then, and slated for a high position in the Air Ministry. Then I heard of his crash in which his best friend had died. The details were scarce, as the papers of Shanghai find cables expensive, but there was a great deal of talk around the tea tables about the accident.

Hampden had taken his friend, Malcolm Redner, for

86

a flight to demonstrate a new type of motor. About two thousand feet over Hanover Airport, the machine had burst into flames and crashed, carrying Malcolm Redner to his death. Hampden had worn a parachute, and had jumped, according to spectators, several seconds before the plane had exploded in the air. Redner, it was said, had not worn a parachute. Then someone had discovered that there was a girl involved. Sheila was her name. Rumor had it that Sheila had been divided in her attentions between Hampden and Redner. There was a court-martial, and an acquittal, but his flight orders were canceled, and an uncle in Parliament had secured a transfer from the RAF into the Navy for Hampden. That was the story I had been hearing for months, and now here was the same Hampden sitting quietly beside me, staring out over the Huangpu. I found myself wondering how such a fine figure of a man could become branded with the names "Coward" and "Murderer."

He must have guessed what I was thinking, for he turned to me and said, "Then you know all about it?"

I stammered for a moment and cursed my lack of wit. "Only one side, sir," I finally got out, "but I hope it isn't the truth."

"Thank you, Ensign. Is this the *Spitfire* on the right?"

The gig thumped against the gangway, letting us step onto the stage. Hampden let me lead the way up the ladder. He waited on the deck while I went to inquire whether the captain would see him. But the captain was asleep, and I showed Hampden to the exec's cabin, so lately vacated by Snyder, who had died upriver. The lieutenant swung his cape from his shoulders across the transom, and for a moment I felt resentment. Snyder's cape had been there all wet with blood and dirty water only a few days before, while Snyder breathed out his death rattle on the bunk. Snyder had been a mighty fine chap, a fighter and a friend of whom anyone might well be proud. That cape of Hampden's was symbolic of the change. One of the finest men who ever trod this earth was replaced with a coward and murderer. But was Hampden all that he had been accused of? I cursed myself for being a blithering idiot and showed the new exec where to stow his dunnage. He had very little to say that night, nor any other night, for that matter, but his eyes spoke that which was in his heart. He was lonely and tired, haggard until his eyes seemed to recede into his skull. I felt sorry for the poor devil.

I didn't get a lot of sleep that night. For one thing, I knew that we were going upriver in the morning, and upriver is the Asiatic synonym for death. But mostly I thought about Hampden. One moment an idol with a million people at his feet, and the next an outcast, a leper, shunned even by his brother officers. I tried to put myself in his place, but found my imagination incapable of the horror such a situation must carry to a man's heart. I lay there in my bunk staring at the beams which were streaked with the blue light of the passageway, a wan, handsome face with a thin scar before my eyes, until I heard the *Spitfire*'s bell strike eight bells, four o'clock, the time for my watch, the dog.

The Huangpu was beautiful in the dawn. The fog of the night before had again been swallowed by the muddy waters, and the brilliant sun of fall crept up over the low horizon to play and dance upon the damp roofs of Shanghai. Two miles down the river lay the main section of the Bund, almost obscured by the thousands of masts which rose out of the sampan and junk anchorage. The British, American, Italian, French and Portuguese men-o'-war looked stern and clean as they swung gently to and fro, straining at their cables as though anxious to be away. Lights flashed off their highly polished brasswork, making what seemed like long strings of sparks. Sailors were busily at work holystoning the already spotless decks and aligning the perfectly kept gear. A few small boats were busy with their small commerce: brown corks prey to the swift Huangpu.

But even as I stood there rapt with the powerful scene, my eyes chanced to rest on a bobbing object a cable length across the stream. I focused my glass upon it, and read there the never-failing message of trouble. A headless corpse was swinging on down to the sea. Turning away from the rail, I called a messenger, instructing him to awaken the captain. I waited for a moment and then turned to pick out the corpse again, but it was gone. The messenger touched my shoulder.

"Sir, the doctor's on duty in the captain's cabin."

I hesitated a moment and left the bridge. The doctor met me at the head of the companionway.

"The captain must be sent ashore immediately." The doctor's eyes rested on the executive officer's cabin door and a fleeting frown passed across his eyes. "He came aboard last night?"

"Yes."

"I don't see why they should wish a rotten beggar like him on the *Spitfire*."

"He seems competent."

"Well, maybe he does. But you mark my words, Ensign, he is no good. What does a flying man know about the Navy?"

"He graduated from the academy five years ago. Educated for the Navy."

"He should be behind bars! Disgrace to the service! Will you call the gig alongside for the captain?" The doctor turned on his heel and went back down the ladder. A second later, Hampden came out of the exec's room. I knew by the look on his face that he had heard every word of the conversation. But he was too much of a gentleman to say anything about it. Instead he walked up to the binnacle and glanced inside at the needle. With one hand on the helm he turned and looked at me.

"Then that means you and I are going upriver together. Will you ask the captain for his keys before they take him ashore? I imagine we'd find it rather hard to get into the chart room lockers without them." He smiled with his mouth. Cold misery was tugging at his eyes.

We weighed anchor at six bells after taking a native pilot aboard and set the course downriver to the junction of the Yangtze and the Huangpu. For an hour we plugged along at fifteen knots past the green banks of the turbulent stream, past the squalid huts which housed their dozens of families, until finally we swung into the channel of the wide Yangtze. In appearance the world was peaceful. Picturesque junks were plying their unwieldy oars with and against the current, and although we narrowly missed several of them as they darted unexpectedly across our bow to foil the river devils, there was a laziness all about which seemed to drug one's senses against the not-far-distant danger.

His Majesty's ship, *Spitfire,* one of many small river gunboats, her stack riddled with small-caliber bullets, her hull dented by more than one high-powered shell, had duties to perform. Her patrol of the river made it safe for the abundant commerce which fed and clothed both Shanghai and China. Men were lying in wait for us up there in the gorges. Dirty men with oddly assorted rifles and uniforms, equipped surprisingly well with light artillery and modern machine guns. In fact, on our last trip, a bos'n had been struck by a bullet from a machine gun of the latest American make. How these modern arms were brought to the brigands was one of our greatest problems.

Lieutenant Hampden, now captain, asked me many questions about these "skirmishes" which plagued the gunboats of six nations, and it seemed to me that he stressed the number of casualties a little more than was necessary. I told him about Snyder, and though it might have been my imagination, I could almost have sworn I saw him shudder. One morning as we sailed up this yellow ribbon of water, I pointed out several of the more conspicuous holes in the stack and began to describe their source. After I had talked a few minutes, I turned to discover that the captain had walked forward and was just entering his cabin.

The effect of his presence was even noticeable in the attitude of the men. They had, of course, heard about Hampden in every grog shop in Shanghai. They seemed a little slow in action when executing his commands, and more than once I heard them growl. But they were trained British sailors, and their captain's word was law, just as a skipper's word has been law from the beginning of the era when Britannia began to rule the waves. He was my superior officer as well as theirs, and for that reason, I gave him every courtesy due a ship's master. He did not seek my company very often, but when he did, it seemed he wanted to talk about the ship or China's puzzling politics. Never did I hear him mention women or England. He ate but little, a cup of black coffee serving as breakfast, a sandwich and a cup of strong tea, his tiffin. I guessed, too, that he slept but little. One morning, early, I passed his room and noticed that his bed was still undisturbed. Another thing caught my attention.

On his locker top there was a picture of a beautiful woman. Her hair was black and her eyelashes long and curving. The picture was a scant three feet away, but I stepped over the jamb and read the inscription, "Love forever, Sheila." I heard a footstep behind me, and turned to stare into the troubled eyes of Hampden.

I expected him to strike me, but his mouth relaxed, and he spoke in a slow voice. "Beautiful, isn't she." I stammered something foolish, but he didn't seem to notice. His eyes were turned inward, "Love—forever." He brushed past me and turned the face of the picture down on the hard metal of the locker.

I scarcely saw him at all during the next few days, except, of course, as we relieved each other on watch. We were standing eight on and eight off, and the strain was beginning to tell. Hampden's eyes grew more sunken, and his face was whiter, if possible, than ever. Murderer and coward! Deserted his friend whom he might have saved. Tired as I was, I often inanely wondered what he would do if I should suddenly hurl those words at his face.

We were entering the gorges above Ki. Day after day had passed almost without incident. We had seen a column of infantry marching peaceably along the shore, and another headless corpse had sped past on its way to the sea, but the closer we came to the danger country, the less we saw of importance. The vigil aboard was beginning to slacken a little. Hampden either didn't notice or didn't care, and I was only an ensign even though I was acting in the capacity of exec. The men had been through too many engagements, and the knife-edge of their keenness had been a little dulled.

But with those tall gorges looking ahead, I began to anticipate trouble. Things were too serene. It was like a calm before a typhoon. The silence was brittle. All morning long, I hadn't seen a single merchant boat. It was not unusual, but at this time it seemed to possess significance.

I was on the bridge writing in the log when it happened. There was a slow scream of a shell turning over and over. The scream became the rumble of a freight train and a huge geyser of yellow water shot up over our stern. A puff of smoke hung in the motionless air at the base of a gorge cliff. The range was less than five hundred yards. The shore was even closer.

Hampden's eyes grew more sunken, and his face was whiter, if possible, than ever. Murderer and coward! Deserted his friend whom he might have saved.

In less time than I could lay down my pen, the hideous clatter of rifle fire burst from the foliage of the bank. My hand went up to the switch, and in a second the huge alarm bell on the bridge was clanging "Quarters!" There was a scurry of feet on the deck as fifty men rushed to their posts. Our machine guns began to rattle. I could see the leaves being stripped from the shrubs on shore. Nowhere did I see Captain Hampden.

I rushed down to his cabin, but even as I touched the door, it opened and he shoved me aside. Buckling on his saber as he ran, he bounded up toward the bridge. One hand caught at the railing. I saw him stiffen. Gray paint flecked off the bulwark at his side. Small holes appeared in the back of his blue coat. His waist bent at a crazy angle and he slumped to the deck.

"Ensign!" he shouted. "Ensign! Get on the bridge! Send me two men!"

I vaulted over his form and jumped up the ladder. Our machine guns were silent. Up forward three men were struggling to swing open the breech of a five-inch. One of them coughed and fell across the stanchion and down into the muddy water. Other men were milling about on the deck. I bawled at them, sent three of them to the machine guns, and two back to Hampden. The pilot was killed. The helm spun and the *Spitfire* yawed helplessly. A shudder ran through her as her bow grounded on a sandbar. Her propellers whirred madly. We were aground in the face of a withering fire. Two men were bringing Hampden onto the deck. He cried for a chair and they set him in one of canvas. Blood was dripping onto the deck.

His eyes stared at the scene before him. He began to shout orders, "Give a hand on that forward gun!" He reached toward the engine room telegraph but couldn't touch the handle. "Full speed astern!" A sailor jumped to do his bidding and the *Spitfire* began to slide off the sandbank. Bullets fell everywhere. They smacked against the superstructure with sledgehammer blows. "Get a crew on that machine gun!" I ran down the ladder, and a second later the gun sputtered into life. The deck was slippery. "Bos'n! See what's the matter with the quarterdeck!" Hampden was bringing order out of the chaos. "Gunner! Spray that clump of trees to the right!" The *Spitfire* was well out in the stream now. "Get on that helm, you!" The ship swung into the current. The five-inch rifles on the afterdeck began to bark. "Ensign! See to the one-pounders." Down in the well deck, I could still hear his voice above the roar of the guns. Another machine gun began to spit lead from our bridge. The firing on shore was slackening. The heavy shells had ceased to hurl water over us. A gray figure slipped out of the shrubs into the water. With a twang of wires, our antennae gave way and writhed upon the deck. I ran back to the bridge. "Swing closer to shore!" The *Spitfire* turned and ran in almost under the muzzles of our unseen enemy guns. "Now, give 'em hell!" Our guns were firing at point-blank range. Gray forms were dropping among the trees. One of our HEs threw geysers of dirt around a one-pounder. "Hand grenades!" Smoke started violently from the ground as AVBs began to find their marks. Then as suddenly as it had begun, it was all over.

Silence was so intense that it hurt. No one was moving on shore, for a look through my glass revealed that there was no one to move. Here and there a machine gun pointed its muzzle to the sky, its crew sprawled in gray clots in the once-green grass. The trees obscured a shambles.

Hampden's head dropped upon his chest, his body twisted half around. A wounded sailor took the helm and we turned our bow downriver.

The doctor came up to the bridge as I was laying Hampden on the deck. He gazed at the prostrate form and then knelt beside him. "No use. Back's broken in three places. Most of his ribs shot away. No use."

Hampden's eyes flickered. "You're right, Doctor. Get to work on those poor devils down below. They're worth saving." His eyes turned on me. "Hit, Ensign?" I told him no. "Then you can take her back upriver . . . again. Don't take me with her. I'd . . . rather not be . . . taken there . . . again. Over there on shore . . . Good place, eh . . . Ensign?" His breath was rasping a little. "Doctor said . . . I was . . . a rotten . . . beggar. Half . . . the world . . . can't . . . be wrong." His head fell forward on his chest again and a little shudder ran through his body. Thin trickles of red were finding their way into the scuppers. "Why should you hate me?" I started to answer, and then realized that he wasn't talking to me. His mind was nine thousand miles away, in England. His voice became strangely clear. "What does 'love forever' mean, Sheila?" He sighed and shuddered again, his head lolling back across my arm. "All right, Malcolm. All right. I hear you. I hear you,

Malcolm Redner. Tell Sheila the truth, Malcolm. Tell her what only you and I know. Tell her, Mal, before it gets too dark. Hear him, Sheila? Hear . . ." He stiffened and raised his head. In his throat there was the hoarse sound I had come to know too well.

Story Preview

Story Preview

NOW that you've just ventured through some of the captivating tales in the Stories from the Golden Age collection by L. Ron Hubbard, turn the page and enjoy a preview of *Cargo of Coffins*. Join Lars Marlin, captain of an oceangoing yacht where his arch-nemesis, Paco Corvino (a man who considers murder a pastime) is aboard. Lars discovers Paco working as the chief steward, but suspects he is up to no good—and their voyage aboard the crowded vessel will likely prove to be a final bloody showdown at sea.

Cargo of Coffins

L ARS drew the .38 up a little, still keeping it out of sight. How he had prayed for this chance! For years without end he had waited patiently to even up a long-standing score.

But with the mud of the swamps of French Guiana hardly dry upon his bare feet, Lars was running a double risk. Any suspicious move from him would bring investigation from the Rio police, and that investigation would send Lars Marlin back to Devil's Island.

His grip tightened upon the .38 and he drew it closer to the torn front of his shirt.

Paco was elegantly dressed as always. Even in French Guiana he had managed to find excellent clothes but now he surpassed himself. His coat was of the best linen and the best cut. His trousers were pressed until the creases were sharp as bayonet blades. His shoes were so white they hurt the eyes on this brilliant tropical day. His cap would have been the envy of a British naval officer, so rakish was its slant, so shiny was its braid.

The insignia was strange to Lars. But it did not matter. Paco was a steward on a yacht, he supposed. But Lars wasted no thought upon Paco Corvino's present. The past was a dull throb in Lars Marlin's brain.

There, jaunty and well fed and reasonably safe, stood Paco, pleased with himself because the Law had just tipped its cap courteously to him. If that officer only knew Paco . . .

Murderer, contraband runner, escaped convict. A man with no more conscience than a bullet, a man cool and deadly, masking a cunning brain with a winning smile.

Oh, yes, Lars Marlin knew all about Paco. It had been Paco who had changed Captain Lars Marlin into Convict 3827645. Paco had done that out of vengeance and now, thought Lars, the tables were turned. One bullet . . .

Lars looked again at the Law under the awning. His gaze went back to Paco and then beyond him, down the cool avenue to tall green and tan palms. Red roofs and white walls. Rugged, pleasant hillsides rising . . .

Once more his hand clenched on the .38. This revenge was sweet enough to repay any consequences. Too long he had dreamed of this moment. He pulled the .38 clear of his shirt, pressing back against the cold, harsh wall. Carefully he leveled the gun. He had no compunctions about the sportsmanship of this. Paco knew that someday Lars Marlin would find him.

The finger began to squeeze down on the trigger.

Laughter nearby jarred Lars Marlin's nerves. The world was ugly to him and this laughter was too gay. Two American girls and a youth had come into the range, approaching the shadowy place where Lars stood.

As the group passed Paco, the blithe Spaniard saluted the man and swept off his cap in a low bow to the ladies.

"Good afternoon, all. Good afternoon, Miss Norton," said the smiling Paco.

Lars looked at Miss Norton. He did not take his eyes away. He could not. It had been long since this homeless American had seen a woman of his own race. And this woman was no usual girl. Her hair was as yellow as the sun. Her graceful body was enough to make de Milo weep from sheer inability to hold those unhampered, lovely curves in marble. Straight and clean and beautiful, she gave the spellbound and unseen Marlin something back, something he had lost in the swelter of heat and the ungodly cruelty of an alien prison camp.

Almost ashamed, he slid the .38 back into his shirt.

Her voice was low and clear. "We sail at midnight, Paco. Make certain you're with us."

"*Yes*, Miss Norton."

The group passed on. They were almost abreast of Lars now. In a moment they would pass within two feet of him. He sensed the presence of her companions but he had eyes only for Miss Norton. He had not heard laughter for years unless it was the wild laughter of madness.

Involuntarily he took off his cap as she passed. A supercilious, patronizing voice brought him back.

"Here, my man."

Silver clinked in Lars Marlin's cap. Blankly he glanced up at the donor. The youth was back between the girls, walking away. Lars looked at the fellow wonderingly. The man had been drinking, as his walk was exaggeratedly straight. Neat and flabby, he had no more character than a dummy outside a clothing store.

Lars Marlin took the *milréis* out of his cap and looked at it. His big, hard mouth curled with contempt. He threw the coin across the walk where an ancient, scabby beggar scooped it up avidly.

Lars looked back at Paco.

Not here. There were other ways. But meanwhile he must not lose the man whom fortune had placed so kindly in his way.

Hesitantly, Lars stepped forward. The hot sun struck his half-bare back and showed the play of muscles through the shredded rag he wore. Beyond him Paco stood looking across the street, jingling coins in his pocket. In profile his face was hawklike and his ivory white teeth flashed like fangs. But, even so, he was pleasant to look upon.

He had been raised on the wharves of world ports without number, foraging with the rats, keeping the society of the drifting flotsam, appearing and disappearing, untraceable. He had developed a smile as armor and it was no deeper than the metal of a salade. And though he did not know his real name he had carefully developed the manners of an aristocrat. It was like Paco to stand in plain sight of the Law, smiling, secure and confident.

Lars came to a heavy stop on Paco's right. They were the same height but there the similarity ended. Lars was built strongly, hewed massively from granite.

Paco looked down at his feet and saw a blue shadow lying there. He saw the breadth of that shadow, how motionless it was, how broad the shoulders were. He saw the outlined tip of an officer's cap.

Paco knew without turning that Lars Marlin, whom he

106

thought to be two thousand miles away in safe confinement, stood with him in the blazing light of the Brazilian sun.

It was not part of Paco's code to show shock. For all he knew, the bullet he so well deserved might be on the verge of an eager trigger. Fear made Paco curl up like burning paper—but only inside. He was sick with nausea and his heart lurched heavily and began to pound in his throat.

Across the street stood the Law, beyond call. Paco must stand there and give no sign.

Only slightly congealed, only a little more false than before, Paco's smile was slowly turned to Lars.

Their eyes clashed. Dark orbs recoiled before the baleful certainty of Norse blue.

To find out more about *Cargo of Coffins* and how you can obtain your copy, go to www.goldenagestories.com.

Glossary

Glossary

STORIES FROM THE GOLDEN AGE *reflect the words and expressions used in the 1930s and 1940s, adding unique flavor and authenticity to the tales. While a character's speech may often reflect regional origins, it also can convey attitudes common in the day. So that readers can better grasp such cultural and historical terms, uncommon words or expressions of the era, the following glossary has been provided.*

---

anchorage: that portion of a harbor, or area outside a harbor, suitable for anchoring, or in which ships are permitted to anchor.

astern: into a position with the stern (the rear part of the ship) pointing in the direction of motion.

auto-da-fé: the public declaration of judgments passed on persons tried in the courts of the Spanish Inquisition, followed by execution by civil authorities of the sentences imposed, especially the burning of condemned heretics at the stake.

AVB: anti-personnel Viven-Bessières rifle grenades, named for the French company that made them. The AVB grenade is fired by means of a sort of cannon that can be fitted to an ordinary rifle. The shell is propelled by the powder in the rifle cartridge.

banshee: (Irish legend) a female spirit whose wailing warns of a death in a house.

barratry: fraud by a master or crew at the expense of the owners of the ship or its cargo.

belay: to secure a rope by turns around a cleat, pin or bitt.

belaying pin: a large wooden or metal pin that fits into a hole in a rail on a ship or boat, and to which a rope can be fastened.

bells: a system to indicate the hour by means of bells, used aboard a ship to regulate the sailor's duty watch. Unlike civil bells, the strikes of the bell do not accord to the number of the hour. Instead, there are eight bells, one for each half-hour of a four-hour watch. Eight bells would be rung at 12:00 midnight, 4:00 AM, 8:00 AM, 12:00 noon, 4:00 PM and 8:00 PM.

binnacle: a built-in housing for a ship's compass.

blue broadside: a forceful verbal attack filled with cursing and swearing.

Borneo: the third largest island in the world, located in southeastern Asia, in the western Pacific Ocean to the north of the Java Sea.

bos'n: bosun; a ship's officer in charge of the supervision and maintenance of the ship and its equipment.

bucko: young fellow; chap; young companion.

bulwark: a solid wall enclosing the perimeter of a weather or main deck for the protection of persons or objects on deck.

Bund: the word *bund* means an embankment and "the Bund" refers to a particular stretch of embanked riverfront along the Huangpu River in Shanghai that is lined with dozens of historical buildings. The Bund lies north of the old walled city of Shanghai. This was initially a British settlement; later the British and American settlements were combined into the International Settlement. A building boom at the end of the nineteenth century and beginning of the twentieth century led to the Bund becoming a major financial hub of East Asia.

cable length: a maritime unit of length measuring 720 feet (220 meters) in the US and 608 feet (185 meters) in England.

cargo boom: a long pole extending upward at an angle from the mast used to load and unload goods.

celluloid collar: removable shirt collars crafted from a material made of white linen and a thin layer of acetate. Introduced in the mid-1870s, they lasted up to five times longer than paper collars and were lighter, more flexible and comfortable to wear.

cheerio: (chiefly British) usually used as a farewell.

Chefoo: the largest fishing port in China's Shandong Province; opened to foreign trade in 1862.

coolyhow: a drink.

cox'n: coxswain; a sailor who has charge of a ship's boat and its crew and usually steers.

crosstree: a horizontal rod attached to a sailing ship's mast to spread the rigging, especially at the head of a topmast.

Dago: San Diego.

davits: any of various cranelike devices, used singly or in pairs, for supporting, raising and lowering boats, anchors and cargo over a hatchway or side of a ship.

Davy Jones: Davy Jones' locker; the ocean's bottom, especially when regarded as the grave of all who perish at sea.

de Milo: Venus de Milo; famous Greek sculpture of Venus, the goddess of love and beauty.

Derringer: a pocket-sized, short-barreled, large-caliber pistol. Named for the US gunsmith Henry Deringer (1786–1868), who designed it.

dog: dog-watch; night shift, especially the last or latest one.

donkey engine: steam donkey; a stationary steam engine used for hoisting or pumping, especially aboard ship.

exec: executive officer; in the navy, the second in command of a ship.

eye: an eye painted on either side of the bow of a ship. The term comes from the ancient custom of painting eyes on the bow so that the ship could see where she was going.

fantail: a rounded overhanging part of a ship's stern (the rear part of the ship).

fidley: an area above ship boilers designed for the intake of fresh air. Fidley grates prevent people or objects from falling into the boiler room.

fireboxes: chambers (as of a furnace or steam boiler) that contains the fire.

flotsam: vagrant, usually destitute people.

fo'c's'le head: forecastle head; the part of the upper deck of a ship at the front. The forecastle is the front of a ship, from the name of the raised castlelike deck on some early sailing vessels, built to overlook and control the enemy's deck.

French Guiana: a French colony of northeast South America on the Atlantic Ocean, established in the nineteenth century and known for its penal colonies (now closed). Cayenne is the capital and the largest city.

Frobisher: Sir Martin Frobisher (1535?–1594), English navigator and among the greatest of Elizabethan seaman. His skills and daring as a seaman brought him a steady rise in rank and by 1565 he had become a captain. He was one of the earliest explorers to seek the Northwest Passage to the Orient and later, as vice admiral, he participated in an expedition, led by Sir Francis Drake, to the West Indies. In 1588 he was knighted for his valiant role in the defeat of the Spanish Armada.

gangway: a narrow, movable platform or ramp forming a bridge by which to board or leave a ship.

gig: a boat reserved for the use of the captain of a ship.

G-men: government men; agents of the Federal Bureau of Investigation.

grog shop: a cheap tavern where alcoholic drinks are served.

half-caste: a person of mixed racial descent.

HE: high explosive; explosive that undergoes an extremely rapid chemical transformation, thereby producing a high-order detonation and shattering effect. High explosives are used as bursting charges for bombs, projectiles, grenades, mines and for demolition.

hearties: sailors.

HMS: His Majesty's Ship.

holystoning: scrubbing the decks of a ship using a block of soft sandstone called *holystone.*

hooker: an older vessel, usually a cargo boat.

Huangpu: long river in China flowing through Shanghai. It divides the city into two regions.

junk: a seagoing ship with a traditional Chinese design and used primarily in Chinese waters. Junks have square sails spread by battens (long flat wooden strips for strengthening a sail), a high stern and usually a flat bottom.

Kanaka: a native Hawaiian.

keel, on an even: steadily; when a ship draws the same quantity of water both at the rear of the ship and forward.

key: a hand-operated device used to transmit Morse code messages.

knot: a unit of speed, equal to one nautical mile, or about 1.15 miles, per hour.

lee rail: a railing on the side of a ship sheltered from the wind; the side opposite to that against which the wind blows.

leeward: situated away from the wind, or on the side of something, especially a boat, that is away or sheltered from the wind.

Lower California: Baja California peninsula; a peninsula in the west of Mexico extending south from the border some 775 miles (1,250 km). It separates the Pacific Ocean from the Gulf of California, a body of water that separates the Baja California peninsula from the Mexican mainland.

men-o'-war: armed ships of a national navy usually carrying between twenty and one hundred and twenty guns.

metal: 1. mettle; substance or quality of temperament; spirit, especially as regards honor and courage. Usually in a good sense; as, to test a person's mettle. 2. mettle; spirited determination.

milréis: (Portuguese) a former Brazilian monetary unit.

Nelson: Viscount Horatio Nelson (1758–1805), British admiral famous for his participation in the Napoleonic Wars. He was noted for his considerable ability to inspire and bring out the best in his men, to the point that it gained the name "The Nelson Touch." He was revered as few military figures have been throughout British history.

one-pounder: a gun firing a one-pound shot or shell. It looks somewhat like a miniature cannon.

plaster saint: a person without human failings. Used sarcastically.

poop deck: a deck that constitutes the roof of a cabin built in the aft part of the ship. The name originates from the Latin *puppis,* for the elevated stern deck.

QST: radio signal meaning "general call to all stations." The Q code is a standardized collection of three-letter message encodings, all starting with the letter "Q"; initially developed for commercial radiotelegraph communication and later adopted by other radio services.

quarterdeck: the rear part of the upper deck of a ship, usually reserved for officers.

quarters: assigned stations or posts; the stations assigned to members of a ship's crew for a particular purpose.

RAF: Royal Air Force.

ratlines: small ropes fastened horizontally between the shrouds in the rigging of a sailing ship to form ladder rungs for the crew going aloft. Also used figuratively.

river devils: According to Chinese superstition, the spirits of the people drowned from time to time in their endeavors to cross the troubled waters. Evil spirits can only move in straight lines, thus one can thwart a river devil or evil spirit by making a sharp turn.

rudder: a means of steering a boat or ship, usually in the form of a pivoting blade under the water, mounted at the stern and controlled by a wheel or handle.

salade: a light, late medieval helmet with a brim flaring in the back to protect the neck, sometimes fitted with a visor.

sampan: any of various small boats of the Far East, as one propelled by a single oar over the stern and provided with a roofing of mats.

Scheherazade: the female narrator of *The Arabian Nights,* who during one thousand and one adventurous nights saved her life by entertaining her husband, the king, with stories.

schooner: a fast sailing ship with at least two masts and with sails set lengthwise.

scupper: to prevent from happening or succeeding; ruin; wreck.

scuppering: sinking a ship deliberately.

scuppers: openings in the side of a ship at deck level that allow water to run off.

scurvy: a disease caused by a deficiency of vitamin C, characterized by bleeding gums and the opening of previously healed wounds. Used as an insult.

scuttle: 1. destroy; wreck. 2. sink a ship by making holes through the bottom.

Seven Great Sea Oaths: an abundance of profanities or swearwords. The Seven Great Seas is in reference to the many seas of the world.

Shanghai: city of eastern China at the mouth of the Yangtze River, and the largest city in the country. Shanghai was opened to foreign trade by treaty in 1842 and quickly prospered. France, Great Britain and the United States all held large concessions (rights to use land granted by a government) in the city until the early twentieth century.

sisal: a strong fiber obtained from the leaves of a plant native to southern Mexico and now cultivated throughout the tropics, used for making rope, sacking, insulation, etc.

slip his anchors: to disengage from the anchors instead of hauling in; get free from the anchor cables.

Spanish Armada: a fleet of about 130 ships that sailed from Lisbon in 1588 to invade England. The Spanish were defeated with approximately 24 ships wrecked off the coast of Ireland with a loss of about 5,000 men.

spiggoties: Spanish-speaking natives of Central or South America who cannot command the English language. It is a mocking imitation of "no speaka de English."

stanchion: an upright bar, post or frame forming a support or barrier.

superstructure: cabins and rooms above the deck of a ship.

telegraph: an apparatus, usually mechanical, for transmitting and receiving orders between the bridge of a ship and the engine room or some other part of the engineering department.

TH: Territory of Hawaii.

tiffin: a meal at midday; a luncheon.

tramp: a freight vessel that does not run regularly between fixed ports, but takes a cargo wherever shippers desire.

transom: transom seat; a kind of bench seat, usually with a locker or drawers underneath.

well deck: the space on the main deck of a ship lying at a lower level between the bridge and either a raised forward deck or a raised deck at the stern, which usually has cabins underneath.

windward: facing the wind or on the side facing the wind.

wing: bridge wing; a narrow walkway extending outward from both sides of a pilothouse to the full width of a ship.

Yangtze: the longest river in Asia and the third longest in the world, after the Nile in Africa and the Amazon in South America.

Yankee: term used by the British to refer to Americans in general.

L. Ron Hubbard
in the Golden Age
of Pulp Fiction

*In writing an adventure story
a writer has to know that he is adventuring
for a lot of people who cannot.
The writer has to take them here and there
about the globe and show them
excitement and love and realism.
As long as that writer is living the part of an
adventurer when he is hammering
the keys, he is succeeding with his story.*

*Adventuring is a state of mind.
If you adventure through life, you have a
good chance to be a success on paper.*

*Adventure doesn't mean globe-trotting,
exactly, and it doesn't mean great deeds.
Adventuring is like art.
You have to live it to make it real.*

— L. RON HUBBARD

L. Ron Hubbard and American Pulp Fiction

B ORN March 13, 1911, L. Ron Hubbard lived a life at least as expansive as the stories with which he enthralled a hundred million readers through a fifty-year career.

Originally hailing from Tilden, Nebraska, he spent his formative years in a classically rugged Montana, replete with the cowpunchers, lawmen and desperadoes who would later people his Wild West adventures. And lest anyone imagine those adventures were drawn from vicarious experience, he was not only breaking broncs at a tender age, he was also among the few whites ever admitted into Blackfoot society as a bona fide blood brother. While if only to round out an otherwise rough and tumble youth, his mother was that rarity of her time—a thoroughly educated woman—who introduced her son to the classics of Occidental literature even before his seventh birthday.

But as any dedicated L. Ron Hubbard reader will attest, his world extended far beyond Montana. In point of fact, and as the son of a United States naval officer, by the age of eighteen he had traveled over a quarter of a million miles. Included therein were three Pacific crossings to a then still mysterious Asia, where he ran with the likes of Her British Majesty's agent-in-place

for North China, and the last in the line of Royal Magicians from the court of Kublai Khan. For the record, L. Ron Hubbard was also among the first Westerners to gain admittance to forbidden Tibetan monasteries below Manchuria, and his photographs of China's Great Wall long graced American geography texts.

L. Ron Hubbard, left, at Congressional Airport, Washington, DC, 1931, with members of George Washington University flying club.

Upon his return to the United States and a hasty completion of his interrupted high school education, the young Ron Hubbard entered George Washington University. There, as fans of his aerial adventures may have heard, he earned his wings as a pioneering barnstormer at the dawn of American aviation. He also earned a place in free-flight record books for the longest sustained flight above Chicago. Moreover, as a roving reporter for *Sportsman Pilot* (featuring his first professionally penned articles), he further helped inspire a generation of pilots who would take America to world airpower.

Immediately beyond his sophomore year, Ron embarked on the first of his famed ethnological expeditions, initially to then untrammeled Caribbean shores (descriptions of which would later fill a whole series of West Indies mystery-thrillers). That the Puerto Rican interior would also figure into the future of Ron Hubbard stories was likewise no accident. For in addition to cultural studies of the island, a 1932–33

LRH expedition is rightly remembered as conducting the first complete mineralogical survey of a Puerto Rico under United States jurisdiction.

There was many another adventure along this vein: As a lifetime member of the famed Explorers Club, L. Ron Hubbard charted North Pacific waters with the first shipboard radio direction finder, and so pioneered a long-range navigation system universally employed until the late twentieth century. While not to put too fine an edge on it, he also held a rare Master Mariner's license to pilot any vessel, of any tonnage in any ocean.

Yet lest we stray too far afield, there is an LRH note at this juncture in his saga, and it reads in part:

"I started out writing for the pulps, writing the best I knew, writing for every mag on the stands, slanting as well as I could."

To which one might add: His earliest submissions date from the summer of 1934, and included tales drawn from true-to-life Asian adventures, with characters roughly modeled on British/American intelligence operatives he had known in Shanghai. His early Westerns were similarly peppered with details drawn from personal experience. Although therein lay a first hard lesson from the often cruel world of the pulps. His first Westerns were soundly rejected as lacking the authenticity of a Max Brand yarn

Capt. L. Ron Hubbard in Ketchikan, Alaska, 1940, on his Alaskan Radio Experimental Expedition, the first of three voyages conducted under the Explorers Club flag.

(a particularly frustrating comment given L. Ron Hubbard's Westerns came straight from his Montana homeland, while Max Brand was a mediocre New York poet named Frederick Schiller Faust, who turned out implausible six-shooter tales from the terrace of an Italian villa).

Nevertheless, and needless to say, L. Ron Hubbard persevered and soon earned a reputation as among the most publishable names in pulp fiction, with a ninety percent placement rate of first-draft manuscripts. He was also among the most prolific, averaging between seventy and a hundred thousand words a month. Hence the rumors that L. Ron Hubbard had redesigned a typewriter for faster keyboard action and pounded out manuscripts on a continuous roll of butcher paper to save the precious seconds it took to insert a single sheet of paper into manual typewriters of the day.

That all L. Ron Hubbard stories did not run beneath said byline is yet another aspect of pulp fiction lore. That is, as publishers periodically rejected manuscripts from top-drawer authors if only to avoid paying top dollar, L. Ron Hubbard and company just as frequently replied with submissions under various pseudonyms. In Ron's case, the list

A MAN OF MANY NAMES

Between 1934 and 1950, L. Ron Hubbard authored more than fifteen million words of fiction in more than two hundred classic publications. To supply his fans and editors with stories across an array of genres and pulp titles, he adopted fifteen pseudonyms in addition to his already renowned L. Ron Hubbard byline.

Winchester Remington Colt
Lt. Jonathan Daly
Capt. Charles Gordon
Capt. L. Ron Hubbard
Bernard Hubbel
Michael Keith
Rene Lafayette
Legionnaire 148
Legionnaire 14830
Ken Martin
Scott Morgan
Lt. Scott Morgan
Kurt von Rachen
Barry Randolph
Capt. Humbert Reynolds

included: Rene Lafayette, Captain Charles Gordon, Lt. Scott Morgan and the notorious Kurt von Rachen—supposedly on the lam for a murder rap, while hammering out two-fisted prose in Argentina. The point: While L. Ron Hubbard as Ken Martin spun stories of Southeast Asian intrigue, LRH as Barry Randolph authored tales of romance on the Western range—which, stretching between a dozen genres is how he came to stand among the two hundred elite authors providing close to a million tales through the glory days of American Pulp Fiction.

L. Ron Hubbard, circa 1930, at the outset of a literary career that would finally span half a century.

In evidence of exactly that, by 1936 L. Ron Hubbard was literally leading pulp fiction's elite as president of New York's American Fiction Guild. Members included a veritable pulp hall of fame: Lester "Doc Savage" Dent, Walter "The Shadow" Gibson, and the legendary Dashiell Hammett—to cite but a few.

Also in evidence of just where L. Ron Hubbard stood within his first two years on the American pulp circuit: By the spring of 1937, he was ensconced in Hollywood, adopting a Caribbean thriller for Columbia Pictures, remembered today as *The Secret of Treasure Island.* Comprising fifteen thirty-minute episodes, the L. Ron Hubbard screenplay led to the most profitable matinée serial in Hollywood history. In accord with Hollywood culture, he was thereafter continually called

The 1937 Secret of Treasure Island, *a fifteen-episode serial adapted for the screen by L. Ron Hubbard from his novel,* Murder at Pirate Castle.

upon to rewrite/doctor scripts—most famously for long-time friend and fellow adventurer Clark Gable.

In the interim—and herein lies another distinctive chapter of the L. Ron Hubbard story—he continually worked to open Pulp Kingdom gates to up-and-coming authors. Or, for that matter, anyone who wished to write. It was a fairly unconventional stance, as markets were already thin and competition razor sharp. But the fact remains, it was an L. Ron Hubbard hallmark that he vehemently lobbied on behalf of young authors—regularly supplying instructional articles to trade journals, guest-lecturing to short story classes at George Washington University and Harvard, and even founding his own creative writing competition. It was established in 1940, dubbed the Golden Pen, and guaranteed winners both New York representation and publication in *Argosy*.

But it was John W. Campbell Jr.'s *Astounding Science Fiction* that finally proved the most memorable LRH vehicle. While every fan of L. Ron Hubbard's galactic epics undoubtedly knows the story, it nonetheless bears repeating: By late 1938, the pulp publishing magnate of Street & Smith was determined to revamp *Astounding Science Fiction* for broader readership. In particular, senior editorial director F. Orlin Tremaine called for stories with a stronger *human element*. When acting editor John W. Campbell balked, preferring his spaceship-driven tales,

Tremaine enlisted Hubbard. Hubbard, in turn, replied with the genre's first truly *character-driven* works, wherein heroes are pitted not against bug-eyed monsters but the mystery and majesty of deep space itself—and thus was launched the Golden Age of Science Fiction.

The names alone are enough to quicken the pulse of any science fiction aficionado, including LRH friend and protégé, Robert Heinlein, Isaac Asimov, A. E. van Vogt and Ray Bradbury. Moreover, when coupled with LRH stories of fantasy, we further come to what's rightly been described as the foundation of every modern tale of horror: L. Ron Hubbard's immortal *Fear*. It was rightly proclaimed by Stephen King as one of the very few works to genuinely warrant that overworked term "classic"—as in: *"This is a classic tale of creeping, surreal menace and horror. . . . This is one of the really, really good ones."*

L. Ron Hubbard, 1948, among fellow science fiction luminaries at the World Science Fiction Convention in Toronto.

To accommodate the greater body of L. Ron Hubbard fantasies, Street & Smith inaugurated *Unknown*—a classic pulp if there ever was one, and wherein readers were soon thrilling to the likes of *Typewriter in the Sky* and *Slaves of Sleep* of which Frederik Pohl would declare: *"There are bits and pieces from Ron's work that became part of the language in ways that very few other writers managed."*

And, indeed, at J. W. Campbell Jr.'s insistence, Ron was regularly drawing on themes from the Arabian Nights and so introducing readers to a world of genies, jinn, Aladdin and Sinbad—all of which, of course, continue to float through cultural mythology to this day.

At least as influential in terms of post-apocalypse stories was L. Ron Hubbard's 1940 *Final Blackout*. Generally acclaimed as the finest anti-war novel of the decade and among the ten best works of the genre ever authored—here, too, was a tale that would live on in ways few other writers

imagined. Hence, the later Robert Heinlein verdict: "Final Blackout *is as perfect a piece of science fiction as has ever been written.*"

Like many another who both lived and wrote American pulp adventure, the war proved a tragic end to Ron's sojourn in the pulps. He served with distinction in four theaters and was highly decorated

Portland, Oregon, 1943; L. Ron Hubbard captain of the US Navy subchaser PC 815.

for commanding corvettes in the North Pacific. He was also grievously wounded in combat, lost many a close friend and colleague and thus resolved to say farewell to pulp fiction and devote himself to what it had supported these many years—namely, his serious research.

But in no way was the LRH literary saga at an end, for as he wrote some thirty years later, in 1980:

"Recently there came a period when I had little to do. This was novel in a life so crammed with busy years, and I decided to amuse myself by writing a novel that was pure science fiction."

That work was *Battlefield Earth: A Saga of the Year 3000*. It was an immediate *New York Times* bestseller and, in fact, the first international science fiction blockbuster in decades. It was not, however, L. Ron Hubbard's magnum opus, as that distinction is generally reserved for his next and final work: The 1.2 million word *Mission Earth*.

> **Final Blackout**
> *is as perfect*
> *a piece of*
> *science fiction as*
> *has ever*
> *been written.*
>
> —Robert Heinlein

How he managed those 1.2 million words in just over twelve months is yet another piece of the L. Ron Hubbard legend. But the fact remains, he did indeed author a ten-volume *dekalogy* that lives in publishing history for the fact that each and every volume of the series was also a *New York Times* bestseller.

Moreover, as subsequent generations discovered L. Ron Hubbard through republished works and novelizations of his screenplays, the mere fact of his name on a cover signaled an international bestseller. . . . Until, to date, sales of his works exceed hundreds of millions, and he otherwise remains among the most enduring and widely read authors in literary history. Although as a final word on the tales of L. Ron Hubbard, perhaps it's enough to simply reiterate what editors told readers in the glory days of American Pulp Fiction:

He writes the way he does, brothers, because he's been there, seen it and done it!

THE STORIES FROM THE GOLDEN AGE

Your ticket to adventure starts here with the Stories from the Golden Age collection by master storyteller L. Ron Hubbard. These gripping tales are set in a kaleidoscope of exotic locales and brim with fascinating characters, including some of the most vile villains, dangerous dames and brazen heroes you'll ever get to meet.

The entire collection of over one hundred and fifty stories is being released in a series of eighty books and audiobooks. For an up-to-date listing of available titles, go to www.goldenagestories.com.

AIR ADVENTURE

133

FAR-FLUNG ADVENTURE

SEA ADVENTURE

TALES FROM THE ORIENT

MYSTERY

FANTASY

SCIENCE FICTION

WESTERN

JOIN THE PULP REVIVAL
America in the 1930s and 40s

Pulp fiction was in its heyday and 30 million readers were regularly riveted by the larger-than-life tales of master storyteller L. Ron Hubbard. For this was pulp fiction's golden age, when the writing was raw and every page packed a walloping punch.

That magic can now be yours. An evocative world of nefarious villains, exotic intrigues, courageous heroes and heroines—a world that today's cinema has barely tapped for tales of adventure and swashbucklers.

Enroll today in the Stories from the Golden Age Club and begin receiving your monthly feature edition selected from more than 150 stories in the collection.

You may choose to enjoy them as either a paperback or audiobook for the special membership price of $9.95 each month along with FREE shipping and handling.